Lola R. Opeye[illegible] in Nigeria and has lived in London, Amsterdam and Kampala.
She is a keen travel and architectural enthusiast and will travel pretty much anywhere for food and pretty buildings.

If you liked my book,
please leave a review
& tell your friends.

Love,
Lola
xoxo

First published in 2020 by Spoken Tree Writing Company.

For permission requests, please write to the publisher at the email address below:
spokentree@icloud.com

Paperback ISBN: 978 1 8381074 2 0

Thank you to Yahweh
for breathing this book into life.

Wrap me in Trees

Lola R. Opeyemi

Part 1, 1992

Chapter 1
Àkúrẹ́, Òndó State, Nigeria

Grace sat in the swivelling office chair. One of the arms was slightly broken, and made a rattling noise as she laid her elbow on it. Eventually, she gave up trying to rest on it and fiddled with it to dissipate her nerves.

Ṣẹ́gun looked up from the carbon paper he was signing, "Mrs Àlejò what can I do for you?"

Grace hesitated, unsure of how to start. She looked around the room, there were plaques and pictures of him everywhere: Ṣẹ́gun Glorious-Johnson – *Housing Officer for the Ministry of Health.*

"It is about our housing, sir."

"Your housing?"

She had been warned he had a habit of repeating the last thing you said. Not letting it get in the way of her aim, she pressed on.

"Yes sir, my family were evicted last night."

"Last night…" Ṣẹ́gun repeated.

"Yes sir," said Grace. "I need your help. I came to see if you can assign us housing in the government quarters, sir."

"Government quarters…" He tapped a biro on the table, "Where is your house now?"

Unsure of how this was relevant, Grace said, "It is on Gbógofọ́lẹ̀ street, sir."

"How many of you in the house?"

"It is my two children and my husband, sir."

"You know we do not allocate those houses to nurses. They are for upper-level civil servants like myself, or the permanent secretaries."

"Yes, sir. It will not be for long, sir. It is only until my husband's business picks up again, sir."

"You're a nurse, abi?"

"Yes, sir."

"I always hear good things about your work, Grace. You are a hardworking woman. But you are only a nurse." He paused to scratch his hoary afro beard, after another thoughtful scratch at his chin, he said, "Come again tomorrow. Let me see if there is something I can do."

Grace left feeling hopeful. She couldn't wait to tell Ernest. She thought about going to his bookstore straight away to tell him the news, but in the end, she changed her mind and decided to walk home. She was on her last five Naira and it was not prudent to spend it on an ọ̀kadà when she could walk and spend the money on tomorrow's breakfast. For tonight, they had some stew left, which they could have with rice.

As she walked home, she thought about how things had changed since she met her dear Ernest. They had been successful once, having married at the tail end of the oil boom. Optimism was high, so they'd had a child. And then another. But as the military government took over, things started to dry up. The first thing to go was the optimism. Then it was the flow of cash.

Ernest had always been proud of not needing the government in his personal business. The changes were gradual at first – little things here and there, then his sales had reduced at the bookstore. First by a hundred Naira month-on-month, then later by much, much more. Still, Ernest did not want to sell the bookstore. It was his pride and joy. Besides, the flexibility meant he could drop off and pick up the kids at their school. They had carried on with no back-up plan.

She knew there was no going back when they had to let go of the househelp. Then they had to hold Ìní back from school. Now, with this eviction, it was time to start looking at other options. Perhaps moving somewhere more stable, more predictable.

Although Ìní was only five, Grace felt guilty at having to hold her daughter back. Grace herself had been held back in her youth in favour of her brothers, and now she had broken her vow to never do that to her own daughter. But Ernest had been right, Ìní was younger and would catch up more quickly than Démì, who was in Primary three, and had started to take more complex things like mathematics, and was more likely to fall behind.

In its prime, the 1960s architecture of the government quarters had looked aspirational and was coveted by the elite civil servants. Now it looked dated, the once pristine cream-coloured terraced bungalows having faded into a dirty mustard from the unpaved roads surrounding the complexes, its low ceilings, small windows, and peeling paintwork making it look older still.

Absurdly enough, the upkeep of the neat hedgerows lining the terraced blocks, to which the gardener, Bàbá Mááshá, tended to once a week, was first rate. Bàbá Mááshá was an old man of indeterminable age who was always good-natured and walked around with his shears, tending to every stray stem daring to poke out from his perfect hedges.

Moving in that night, the children were excited as it was slightly larger than their old place. They ran around exploring, with Ìní declaring she liked the smell of their new house. Démì ran around the rooms scoping out new nooks for their hide-and-seek games, plotting ahead so he could get the upper hand in future games.

The next day, the family sat in their new living room. It was a Sunday afternoon, that non-time between lunch and dinner where an ẹ̀bà-induced food coma had pushed the family into collective tiredness. Grace turned to Ernest and said, "Things aren't getting better, are they?"

Assuming guilt for how things were going in the family, Ernest spoke quietly. "Things will pick up."

"Ernest ọkọ mi," she said, "things are very unpredictable for us." She used his nickname when she wanted to persuade him of something. "We never know when the government is going to pay my salary, the book shop is unpredictable. At least if one of us goes abroad… I hear they are hiring nurses in the UK. We can at least..." Grace stopped herself as she clocked Ernest's discouraging shoulder tilt; he often did that when he thought something was a bad idea.

"And what about our children?" he said, "Who is going to take care of them?"

"Ernest, you know I can take care of them if I'm the one staying. Or if you are the one staying, you are more than capable."

Ernest was proud she had said that. He prided himself on not being like most of his friends who had no interest in how their children were raised. *It's a woman's job*, they would say. But Ernest loved spending time with his children and seeing how they were doing. Ernest had emerged out of a broken childhood, his emotions all bent out of shape, with rough edges. But in the midst of that brokenness, he had found the right tools through education to get through. He had always thought no matter what, he would try to give his children a good education. It broke his heart that they had to hold Ìní back in preference for money and food. Grace knew how to get to his soft heart, and he realised she was right. They needed another plan.

This was how the Àlejòs started planning one more move that would change their lives; it was six years before the whole family would find themselves in the UK. But they would move two more times before that.

Àkúrẹ́ was a dusty town, with low-level buildings. There was no industrial centre as such but rather one could argue it had three centres. There was the commercial centre on hospital road, so called because it had the central hospital; there was the immigrant shops on Àràkálẹ̀ road where the Igbo merchants sold everything from footwear to plastic plates and hair extensions, and the Hausa merchants sold and repaired everything watch-related. Then there was Ọba Adéṣidà road, which housed the palace and the central mosque – this was where the market women sold everything from tomatoes to canned goods and this was the place where Ernest had his store – Promise Bookshop – his pride and joy.

Ernest was deprived of a good education so he became obsessed with books, outside of the school there were no formal libraries so he dedicated himself to picking up books, from the streets and from abandoned newspapers left by the street vendors.

He became an avid reader, and with his wide-ranging interests (and a lot of luck) he had educated himself into a job on the sales floor with the post-colonial monolith that was the United Africa Company (or "the UAC"). That was in the 1970s.

But after the oil boom and the heady days of post-independence success, came mismanagement by the military government, which had led to austerity. He had lost his job at the UAC.

With Grace's encouragement, he had used his experience in sales to start a bookstore. He had cobbled money together from his savings and the rest he borrowed from Simon. It was now a few years into his bookstore business, and although it had started out well, it had not taken off as he had hoped.

The economy was bad and school funding was drying up, which meant parents were spending less on books, and taking a chance on their children sharing books with the rich kids in their class.

Corruption was persistent and there had been no government turnover in many years. No one could see a way out.

Now, sitting behind the counter at his bookstore on a hot and slow afternoon in May, Ernest looked out into the busy street on Ọba Adéṣidà road and tried to imagine having to let his place go. But he couldn't. Not yet. He knew he would have to eventually. It made too much sense. They had decided Grace had a better chance of getting a visa if she tried the nursing route, and they would need the money for her ticket and the first few months of her settling in.

Ernest sighed loudly. The sweat trails running down his back bringing him back to the present, reminding him of the lack of air conditioning in the store. He decided to go buy some cold water. He called out to the street vendor stationed outside.

"Ebenezer, can you watch the shop while I go get ice water?" Ebenezer had roasted corn and bọ̀lè on that corner for almost a decade, everybody knew him. Back when Ernest had first opened the store, he had indulged in some of Ebenezer's delicately charred corn or sweet plantain treats daily, but these days he tried to keep his hunger repressed until he could eat with his family in the evenings.

Not much was likely to happen while he was gone anyway. He hadn't had customers for days. He decided to only close the front metal bar gate, leaving the internal wooden door ajar so customers could see he was still open for business.

Ernest made his way down to the market. At first, he headed for the snacks and drinks shop nearby, but as he got closer, he remembered the woman who owned it was rather ornery and her stuff was pricey too. He made a U-turn, deciding to walk down towards the main market. He hated the chaos of the open-air market, but it was cheaper.

As he walked in the midday heat, he rubbed his bald patch which was now starting to tingle and he quickened his steps; he spotted a young boy of not more than twelve, yelling *Ice water tútù ré*, followed by a piercing whistle. Taking advantage of the convenience, Ernest stopped him and bought some cold water. He could smell kúlí-kúlí nearby and turned to look, his stomach rumbling in anticipation of the fried peanut snack. He tried to resist, he would save the money instead. His family needed it – he hadn't made a sale this week.

He went back to the bookstore and waited out the rest of the afternoon. Nearer to closing time, someone came in to buy pencil sharpeners; they tried to haggle, which irritated him, but he remained polite.

As he closed out that evening, as he thought of potential buyers, he mentally began to say goodbye to his beloved store. By the time he got into his car, he had changed his mind again. He lived in hope that things would get better in his country.

Ernest's daily arrival at home from his bookstore was unmistakeable. Grace could always hear the tin-like sounds of the Ìjàpá before it then emerged in a billow of smoke, with Ernest folded in behind the wheel. Simon had nicknamed it Ìjàpá because of the Volkswagen Beetle's distinct tortoise shape, partly to make fun of Ernest, but it had been so funny that Ernest had not been offended and the nickname had stuck. Plus, it made the children laugh to think they were being carted around in a tortoise shell.

As Ernest pulled in to the driveway, Démì and Ìní rushed out to meet him as always. Grace smiled to herself as she watched this daily routine; she sat back in the living room and watched through the window their display of adoration for their dad. It was always the same: first, they took his briefcase, and then they searched inside, Démì looking for snacks and Ìní for books. Today, Ernest had neither.

Ernest walked into the house with Ìní and Démì trailing behind him, Grace enjoyed the contrast of how little they were next to him.

Ernest was very tall, and he left most people in his wake by taking giant strides ahead of them. It was his humble but confident stride that first attracted her to him, although his once glorious afro had now given way to a bald patch. With her, over the years, he'd learned to match her hurried but nimble pace, as she hurried through life to make up for her short legs.

Ernest kissed Grace hello, she was now sitting in her favourite corner on the sofa. He studied her quietly. She had small almond-shaped eyes that narrowed even further whenever she smiled, showing off her high cheek bones and dimpled cheeks. He loved watching her laugh. She had thin limbs that narrowed into elegant wrists and long narrow fingers. She was endlessly elegant.

When he'd first met her, she wore her hair in a Jheri curl and carried her activator gel everywhere. At one point, in their early days of dating, she had left her activator gel on the sink in his bathroom and he thought it was deliberate so she could come back. It had turned out it was an accident. Instead of mentioning it, he waited. He didn't want to seem too eager.

When she found out he had had it all along, she was annoyed with him, he'd never been more terrified or excited, she was beautiful when angry – her eyes dramatically widening to show their full almond shape. He'd come to learn this outburst was a rare occurrence, Grace communicated economically, quietly making her point and only saying what she needed to.

At dinner that evening, sitting opposite him at the other end of their dining table, she smiled exposing her dimples as she watched Démì quietly and diligently pick out the fish bones in his meal.

Ìní complained about the bones and refused to eat, "You'll eat what we have. Some people have nothing to eat!" Ernest and Grace chastised, almost in unison, a well practised verse in their home.

After dinner, they discussed their next move, and whom they could approach to buy the bookstore.

———

Grace, a laconic woman of great intelligence had been a government scientist in the early 1970s, defying the odds of not being educated by her father. "You're just a girl," he would say. "When you marry I will lose all the money I have spent on you to your husband's house."

Thus, he had refused to educate her, spending all his money on her brothers. Grace's mother, a short but renegade woman, also of great intellect, had used her own money from selling tomatoes in the market to educate Grace in secret. Seeing Grace's potential early on, her mind quick in solving household quarrels or when helping with their budgetary needs, she had enrolled Grace in the local village primary school, which took place on a bench in Auntie Winifred's backyard with six other girls with equally renegade mothers. That was how Grace got her primary school education.

Her natural abilities had led her to attend secondary school via a scholarship, where subsequent scholarships meant that her mother no longer needed to keep petty cash aside to privately educate her in Auntie Winifred's backyard.

Grace had fond memories of Auntie Winifred's makeshift school, but most vividly, she remembered being covered in white dust from Auntie Winnie's enthused and frequent wiping of the chalkboard.

Meeting Ernest in the late 70s had been a revelation for Grace. She had never met anyone who loved education like her. Theirs was a natural and still evolving love. Ernest, the avid reader, and Grace the quiet observer. Her sharp mind, although taciturn in its nature, was a good contrast to Ernest's verbose one. It was a contrast that would carry them through many years of good and bad.

Grace now worked as a nurse for the Ministry of Health in Àkúrẹ́ (a government department known for being corrupt and opaque in a sea of impenetrable bureaucracy), her hardworking and fastidious nature surpassed only by her notoriety as a former scientist at the prestigious University College Hospital "UCH" in Ibadan.

After the lab got defunded, equipment repairs tailed off and hospital payments became few and far between, if at all; the lab had closed, to Grace's disheartenment. Ever a survivor, Grace parlayed this into a nursing career.

Things were tough on the family now but Grace had figured out a way to economise. Her salary was swallowed up by their biggest expense, rent. On weekdays, they had one meal a day at dinner time and the kids ate lunch at school.

They shared communal meals from one pot, although at special times of the year (and when they could afford more), the children got their own plates, which they didn't seem to like as much as they loved sharing.

A surprise expense — like if the Ìjàpá broke down — may mean that they would have garri for a few days, but Grace used this a last resort as she thought there was very little nutritional value in processed cassava.

As they planned their next move, and in case she got the visa, Grace started a list for Ernest. A list of the things she did that he didn't see.

In contrast to the heaving streets of Lagos, the atmosphere at the embassy was intimidating and pristine. There was a palpable but muted energy, a mixture of the intimidating self-importance of the embassy staff and the fermenting sweat of the nervous visa-seekers as they filed in from the heat into the cool air inside.

They both felt nervous and tired, which compelled Ernest and Grace to speak in hushed tones. They had already sold the Ìjàpá to pay for their visa fees, getting up before the sun to take the six-hour bus ride to the embassy.

Now Grace was fussing with a stain on her blouse, *I must've sustained it from the bus ride*, she thought. Public transport could be unpredictable, if it wasn't the rich-red dust forming shapes on your well pressed clothes, it was the jagged edges from panel-beaten cars ripping holes in them.

Finally, it was their turn. A young man in police uniform called them in, Grace felt like her heart stood up within her chest and started racing. Ernest wiped down the sweat running down from his bald spot down his neck. They filed into the embassy official's room.

"Good morning, sir."

"Good morning, Mr and Mrs Aleyjo."

Correcting the British officer, Ernest said, "It's Àlejò," emphasising the musical monophthong doh-ray-doh sounds.

"I'm sorry for the mispronunciation," the official said but he did not attempt to mimic Ernest's pronunciation. "My name is Mr Rawlings, I am in charge of your visa application. Thank you for coming in for this interview. Mrs Aleyjo, what is your purpose for wanting to visit the UK?"

The air conditioning was making Grace's sweat-drenched limbs turn into icy tentacles, she sat on her hands to warm herself. "For study, Mr Rawlings… to study," Grace stuttered back.

"I see from your application you have two small children?"

"Yes, they are five and seven, sir."

He flipped through the file in front of him, the hum of the air conditioner now the loudest thing in the room.

Afterwards he looked up, "So why do you want to come to the UK when you have two small children?"

"To advance my career opportunities. There is a letter from the Minister for Health in there to say which courses I am going to do."

"Yes, I see it here," he replied, pulling out a typewritten piece of paper and running his eye over it, mouthing the words on the page. "You see, I just don't believe it. I'm afraid we have to reject your visa application. I'm sorry, Mrs Aleyjo."

Chapter 2

"What do I know about the Caribbean?" Grace complained sceptically to Ernest.

"Let's just try it. He said we won't need a visa if we go somewhere like Barbados or Jamaica. All we need to do is buy a ticket, from there you can make your way to London," Ernest pressed.

"We've already lost money on the Ìjàpá. Where will we find money for a ticket to the Caribbean?" Grace was feeling the full weight of their disappointment with the visa, like someone had quietly and deliberately excavated her innards leaving her hollow yet still holding the broken shell of her dreams.

"We still haven't sold the bookshop. Let's find a buyer for the bookshop," Ernest said gently.

"I thought we agreed to wait to sell the bookshop. What will you do while I am gone?"

Finally used to the idea of letting go of the bookstore Ernest said, "Simon is always telling me to join him in the state contracting business. He makes good money. It is flexible. It will allow me to take care of the kids while you are gone. Look, it worked for the Adélékès, Marion went to Jamaica and got a visa immediately, and now she's been working for six months and she has been able to help send money for the children's school fees."

"It's just I'm feeling discouraged, Ernest." Grace put her head in her hands and leaned forward in despair. They had no money, no car, and they had just lost a small fortune trying to get a visa.

"Don't be discouraged. Let's try again. I really believe in these kids. If they can get a good education, they will not have to struggle like we did. Right now, we have no other options."

Ernest hugged her tightly and Grace surrendered herself to his embrace.

Ernest went to see his friend, Simon, who had many contacts in government and who for the last decade had been able to supplement his modest income from his electronics store with state contracts. Simon boasted that a ten percent cut on supplying plates to seventeen hospitals had netted him enough money to pay his children's school fees for a whole term. Ernest was impressed with the returns but he was reticent in dealing with the government – things could be unpredictable, and it was hard to stay honest.

Still, his friend convinced him to try a small contract and see how it went. "Start *small* small… like next week, I have to go to the port to clear some government imports. Come with me and you can see how it works."

Ernest was never sure how much he could trust Simon's word.

Still, and despite his shifting-sands personality, Simon had been a good friend to him over the years, and

Ernest decided it was a good idea to follow him to the port on Monday.

———

Ernest and Grace visited Alhaji E.O.D. to see if he would be willing to buy Promise Bookshop. Despite his bookstore-mogul persona and devout Muslim cover, Alhaji E.O.D. was notoriously sleazy. He had multiple wives who all worked in his store. They all bleached their skin, and each new wife was younger and lighter than the last.

His father had started E.O.D. Books in pre-independence Nigeria by selling English-language books, with the store later expanding into pan-African fiction, and eventually becoming the go-to store for Nigerian-language fiction.

E.O.D. stood for 'End of days', a testimony to the older Alhaji's fascination with all things apocalyptic, but when his son took over he changed it to E.O.D. Books, figuring his father's dour rhetoric was bad for business.

E.O.D. Books was a grand, four-storied building on the outskirts of Àkúrẹ́, but as the city expanded it had become part of what was now considered the centre of the city.

Alhaji E.O.D. was in fact an Igbo salesman from Imo State, but he self-styled as an Alhaji to curry favour with the Muslim population in the area where his shop was. His real name was Sam Okoro; neither he nor his father were Muslim, and neither had undertaken the holy pilgrimage to qualify for the title. Some had heard the mercenary tale about the spurious title, but no one dared question his piety.

On their way to their first negotiation with Alhaji E.O.D., the Àlejòs met his first son; he was smoking outside the bookstore. He gave them a short, yet slightly obsequious, greeting.

"Pẹ̀lẹ́, where is your father?" Ernest said.

"In his office, sir. I will take you." Junior led them up the stairs to the second floor; as they walked down the hallway they could hear Alhaji E.O.D. arguing with a woman. When they knocked on the door, out came Kalifatu, Alhaji's latest wife. She curtsied slightly in deferential greeting to Ernest and Grace.

"Ernest, Ernest, come in. Welcome to my shop," spreading out his arms, Alhaji embraced Ernest and ignored Grace. "Please sit down."

Alhaji agreed to buy the bookstore and pay in three instalments of 30%, 40%, and 30%, where the physical ownership of the bookstore would transfer to Alhaji when he had paid 70%.

To seal the deal, and as a sign of their new friendship, Alhaji E.O.D. gave Ernest a small goat and a chicken, and instructed some of his younger sons to help load them into the taxi that was to take Grace and Ernest home.

———

Grace was hungry again. She wondered how the children felt. They had only had a bit of rice and stew left tonight, so she and Ernest had decided to go without and give the stew to the children. There was no meat left, but they boiled the last two eggs and added them to the stew.

On such nights, when there was no food, Grace would eat a piece of chili from the storage tray, the ensuing burn making her drink lots of water – it was usually enough to keep hunger at bay until the morning. Usually. But not tonight. Nightmares about hunger tormented her, punctuated by short spells of deep sleep.

She woke up from chasing a chicken thigh, which had retaliated by growing feet and chasing *her*; as she'd rounded a corner seeking solace there were more chickens waiting, dressed as runners.

She was now wide awake. Her feet cold and feeling like lead. She looked over at Ernest – he was fast asleep. Somehow, he was always able to handle hunger better than her.

She worried about tomorrow, what they would eat. As her mind paced back and forth, she fell asleep again, and dreamed of a better life.

———

Grace sat Démì down in the living room. Ernest had subtly disappeared into the other room. He was reading the newspaper.

Ìní had sensed something was up and didn't want to participate in whatever discussion her mother was gearing herself up for. When called, she sat quietly on the other edge of the sofa and stared at her mother through her interlaced fingers. She was playing hide and seek but in plain sight.

How do I say this without falling apart? Grace thought. She had been crying all morning and been comforted by Ernest. We're doing this for them, he would say, rubbing her back gently and trying not to cry himself.

"My darlings, Mummy is going abroad," began Grace.

"What does abroad mean?" asked Démì.

"Abroad is ìrìnàjò, journey, I'm going to London," Grace said.

"London," they chorused. Having seen that Sesame Street episode about the letter L, and knowing that London was in England and so far away, you could only get there by aeroplane, the children were excited.

"When will you come back?" Ìní asked having fully forgotten her sulk and realising the gossip at play was not a sad thing at all but a rather exciting thing that would happen to her mother.

"I don't know. Maybe one year or two. I will try to come back as soon as possible," said Grace softly.

"So, you'll be like Fisáyọ̀'s mum," Démì said, mentioning one of the minister's children at his school, whose wife's frequent shopping trips to London was notorious. "Yesterday, he had a new pencil case and bag," Démì continued. "Maybe you can also buy me a pencil case, he's the only one that has one."

"Well, I'm going for a different reason, darling. We sometimes can't afford to keep you both in school at the same time because I don't always get my salary or when Daddy hasn't sold enough books. If I work abroad, I will get paid more regularly and we can afford to keep you both in school so Ìní can go back next term."

"I also want a new pencil case and bag o," Ìní said.

Grace wanted to cry at their enthusiasm, now realising they didn't fully understand what was happening. Her heart was breaking but she hid it.

She left them watching TV and as she exited the room, Ernest, having heard all the excitement from the other room, was waiting there with open arms. She collapsed into his arms and sobbed until she had no more tears.

"Ah Uncle, Auntie! Welcome, let me get you some Fanta or Vimto," Ànú Tìmáyọ̀ still referred to Grace and Ernest as Uncle and Auntie despite only a one-year age gap. Grace had been her senior in high school and as was their custom then, you referred to everyone in the classes above as 'Auntie' or 'Senior'. "Dalos is still in the clinic, he should be finishing soon then he can join us for dinner." She sat down fussing with her skirt, it was rumpled on the bottom left. She was always a nervous sort, Grace remembered from their school days how Ànú would wring her hands nervously each time someone addressed her directly.

In walked Dalos in a cloud of pungent cologne, a poor attempt to mask the musty smell from his windowless office. When he had been holed-up with patients, he sometimes came in to dinner smelling… less than fresh. Ànú helpfully left several aftershaves by the door connecting his clinic to the main house. Today, he had picked '*Musk* by Alati'. Ànú had found it in Peckham on one of her travels to the UK.

Dalos was a light-skinned man with a dark-brown mole on his left cheek. One of his eyes was bigger than the other, yet he carried himself with the panache of someone who knew he was good looking, and he was. He hugged his dear friend Ernest hello, their towering height meeting in an enthusiastic hug. Then he turned to give Grace a short hug.

"Sorry I was late. I was operating on a pregnant goat. Long time, Ernest! How's business?"

"Business is good o. Although we have now sold it. That's actually why we came here, for some advice. Grace is going abroad. We want to get out and do something for our children. The future is looking uncertain with this economy, it's getting harder to eat and I don't see a bright future for these children."

"Ah ah, it's not that bad," said Dalos.

"Last week, there was a fuel shortage so there was no taxi to take Démì to school and this week there is petrol but I cannot afford it," said Ernest.

"My friend, if you had told me I would've helped."

"How many times will I be calling you to help me?"

"We want to go somewhere where things are more predictable. I cannot remember the last time they paid my salary," Grace added. "We have heard they're looking for nurses in the UK and we've seen some people from the ministry who have left and they're making it. We want to try too. See if there's another way. I'm tired of watching my children go hungry."

"Ah I didn't know it was that bad," Dalos said.

"My friend, you have connections. You have your clinic. You don't depend on government salary. In fact, your biggest customer is the ministry of Health and Agric so it is like you are protected from the daily sufferings," Ernest said.

"Which is why you should ask me for help now. I would have helped you. So, what is your plan?" Dalos said.

"Grace will go first and see if she can get a good job, and we can see about the rest of the family joining later," said Ernest.

"I will tell you this, I cannot lie to you my friend. I know the UK, I studied there. This will be very disruptive for your children if your wife is there and you are here. Who is going to take care of your children?"

"Me, of course. What do you mean?" Ernest said.

"I mean when was the last time you washed your children's clothes or cooked something in the kitchen?"

"Ernest cooks o!" Grace interjected. "He's not like the men in my father's generation who don't know where the kitchen is."

"Your father's generation," Ànú scoffed. "Try this generation. Dalos only knows how to eat food, he doesn't know where it comes from."

"Do you know where the money for the food comes from?" Dalos retorted. "I was elbow-deep in a goat today. No, you never ask. But you know how to spend the money."

At this, Ànú got up and wandered into the kitchen, muttering something about needing to go and yell at the housegirl to bring in dinner.

Dalos continued, "We are just managing here ourselves. The clinic is barely making ends meet but it is better than going somewhere and starting again. Don't go. Do not do this to your children. You will regret it."

Ànú came back in, housegirl in tow and carrying a large tray.

As they sat down to eat, Ernest broached the topic again, "Deji has gone, him and I started together at the UAC back in the day. After the company closed he couldn't find another job, so he moved to England five years ago. Last time I saw him, he was looking good, he had starch on his clothes. He told me life was hard but good. It was more predictable. You work, they pay you. This unpredictability is not good for my children. Ìní is not currently in school. We can't afford it. It was either that or no food for a few weeks. Thank God she is young enough to not miss much of the curriculum, and that is when we have the school fees…" Ernest ran out of steam and he stopped to heap some rice onto his spoon.

Grace added, "With what they say, there is a real shortage of nurses there, if I can find work, it is good money. I can send money home for the children for their school fees, and whatever Ernest is making from the contracting will be enough for their food and rent."

"What contracting?" Ànú asked.

"His friend Simon knows some people in government who can help him with supply chain work," said Grace.

"Have you got a visa yet?"

"No…," Ernest paused, knowing what was likely coming. "We were rejected for a visa," he added quietly, somewhat embarrassed.

"Ah!" Dalos and Ànú chorused, then looked at each other.

"I can't believe you're leaving your children like this," Ànú said.

"The way I see it, it's either we all starve together or I leave and they live," Grace responded sharply.

After a few moments of silence, Ernest now realising that sharing their dream with their friends was perhaps, in retrospect, not a good idea, he added softly, "Grace will go to Barbados and apply from there. She does not need a visa to go there. So, we have bought a ticket for Barbados."

"If that doesn't work?" Dalos said.

"Then she will come back. Her job will still be at the ministry."

On the drive to the airport, Ernest was nervous. He was very quiet. Grace figured he was just concentrating. They had borrowed Simon's car: it had stubborn brakes so you had to really lean on it plus the clutch was equally recalcitrant. It made her think of the Ìjàpá with its little quirks too.

She didn't know what to expect of the journey ahead, but she knew it was a positive chance to turn the family's situation around.

The journey to the airport was uneventful. As they said their goodbyes at the airport, the kids were chipper, "Mommy's going to London," they both chanted.

On the drive back to Àkúrẹ́ the next day, the kids started complaining about being hungry, so Ernest got them some *Gala* from the street vendors, which they ate and promptly fell asleep. Ernest did not much like the meaty snacks himself to he munched on some nuts to keep himself awake.

It was Saturday, so Ernest took them by the bookstore instead of going straight home. He needed a distraction. As he opened the shop, Ìní skipped up the steps, excited to be in her favourite place. She went to the corner where Ernest stored the damaged books and flipped through anything for Primary Two.

Démì didn't enjoy the bookstore as much as Ìní, but he loved sitting with his father; he sat on the high stool that Ernest had bought for him specially, his eyes reaching the tall desk. They sat and talked about Proverbs, Ernest's favourite topic. Later on, Ernest got them some dinner of bọ̀lè and groundnut from Ebenezer.

It was the oddest sensation, looking like everybody yet not being able to identify with them. She almost wanted to speak Yorùbá to people, and sometimes she did, only to correct herself at the last minute and switch to English. Grace did not miss the split-second adjustments people had to make when they heard her accent and tried to place where she was from and what she was doing there. She did not have the cavalier air of someone on holiday, and she certainly wasn't dressed like the ones in a perpetual bathing suit and flowing kaftan. So, they wondered, and, sometimes, they asked, but she kept her answers vague.

Grace tried to stay inconspicuous in the resort grounds, unless she was stepping outside to make calls in the public phone box.

The day came when the bus came to cart them to the visa office. Olúyẹdé, their contact in Barbados, had come that morning during breakfast to warn them that a load of people had been rejected at the embassy the week before. The embassy had discovered that, despite embargoes in their home country, people were still trying to use Barbados as a way to get into England. However, he was still willing to take anybody who was willing to risk it. Grace was willing. To go back was not an option.

So that afternoon, when the bus came, some of Grace's travel mates decided to stay behind because of this news.

The journey on the bus was tense. Olúyẹdé sat in front in his usual topless uniform, whistling off-pitch. The hairs underneath Grace's wig stood up in irritation. Someone behind her kissed their teeth pointedly. Still the whistling continued. Resigning herself to bearing with the whistling, Grace tried to will her nerves away. She leaned forward with her chin in her hands, rocking side to side with the rhythm of the bus, she tried to focus her mind.

Finally, the whistling stopped. They had reached the embassy.

Chapter 3

Grace landed in London on a cold October morning. She was picked up by her cousin, Tómi.

Tómi lived with her husband, Fẹ́mi, on quiet, mansion-lined Hollyfield Road in Kensington. It was a three-storied house painted in all white and surrounded by manicured lawns. There was a basement floor, which housed a large swimming pool on one side and a fleet of cars on the other.

The only thing Grace knew about Fẹ́mi was that he was a politician turned billionaire, and no one knew how he had come about his fortune.

"Thank you my sister for picking me up. How is Tóbi and the twins?"

"Tóbi is a handful o, but the twins are doing well." Tómi said. "Very well," she added after a short pause.

From what Grace remembered from their youth, Tómi had the kind of disposition where you couldn't always tell what she was thinking, which made her slightly unpredictable. She could be very kind when she was paying attention, and at other times, she managed to exude a certain joylessness about life.

"Fẹ́mi nko?" Grace said.

"He's fine. Business is booming."

At this Grace fell silent. Any follow-up questions could lead them both to embarrassment since neither Tómi nor Fẹ́mi had ever revealed what exactly it was

Fẹ́mi did. Any questions were usually followed by a loud silence and some gentle feet shuffling.

Tómi and Fẹ́mi had three boys: sixteen-year-old Tóbi and five-year-old twin boys – Táyé and Kẹ́hìndé. Grace had met Tóbi once when he was ten years old and Tómi had brought him to their house in Àkúrẹ́ one summer. He had sat sulkily for the whole afternoon, complaining about the flies and the lack of air-conditioning.

As Tómi took her around the Kensington mansion, Grace noticed several security staff, including two in the windowless basement who guarded the cars and, presumably, the swimming pool. Tómi did not introduce her to the staff, but Grace tried to greet all of them.

Later, in the living room, Tómi picked up the intercom and spoke quietly to summon Sylvia the househelp.

"So, what are your plans while you are here? How are you going to find work?" Tómi said in her characteristic quiet voice.

"As from tomorrow, I will start applying for nursing jobs in hospitals. Do you know how I can call Ernest to tell him I have landed?"

"Well you can't use the phone, it's expensive, but tomorrow you can buy a phone card and call him," Tómi responded.

"What is a phone card?"

Before Tómi could respond, Fẹ́mi came in. He was a rotund man in his mid-forties. He was wearing a closely fitted white vest, which made his belly hang over his tiny shorts. Tómi looked annoyed at the interruption.

Fẹ́mi noticed Grace sitting opposite his wife, "Auntie Grace," addressing her in the polite sister-in-law Yorùbá way. "When did you arrive?"

"Just this morning, Tómi picked me up. Thank you for letting me stay here."

"You're welcome." Turning his attention to Tómi, he said, "Has anyone seen Tóbi? That useless boy, sometimes I don't see that boy for days. Our house is too big, you know? Did Tómi show you around? What do you think? We are thinking of raising the back garden and adding a stage for when Tómi is doing gbéborùn in her women's meetings."

Tómi's response was to look down at the slight.

To fill the silence, Grace muttered something in defence of Tómi not being that much of a busybody by nature, then Fẹ́mi excused himself and left the room.

She did not get to ask Tómi about the phone card again. Tómi rushed out shortly after for the rest of the day, muttering something about picking up the kids from school. Grace didn't know how to tell her it was a Saturday.

———

Grace was up early the next morning. She did not sleep well because she had not called Ernest and she knew he would have been worrying.

She left her room, and tried to make her way downstairs, but she couldn't remember the way – too many hallways and nooks. As she rounded the corner at the end of the long hallway, she ran into the twins, sitting side-by-side in a colourful toy car.

"No, you push it!"

"It's my turn," they argued between them.

She couldn't tell them apart yet so she called out the Yorùbá name for the first twin, "Táyé!"

The twins, having long enshrouded themselves in the mystery of both answering to either name, looked up in response. Confused, Grace continued, "Can you show me the living room?"

"Ok, auntie," they chorused and leapt off the toy car, running down the stairs singing a nursery rhyme in unison.

Beyond the living room, she could hear sounds in the kitchen. She entered to find Sylvia bent over the cooker, giving it a good scrub and singing *Jehovah is your name.* She greeted her in Yorùbá, in her attempt to be informal then asked about the phone card.

"Auntie, I no fit speak Yorùbá, I dey from Calabar, if you waka go cornershop, at de end of de street, you fit dey buy phone card."

Embarrassed at her assumption, Grace apologised and left the kitchen with a quiet 'thank you' to Sylvia.

After buying the phonecard, Grace approached the only phone box on the street. It was opposite the corner shop, it had been vandalised slightly with its door askew, otherwise it was clean and looked presentable. She read the instructions on the phonecard, scratched the shaded silver pane to reveal the code, and began to dial. She was calling their neighbour, Ṣọ̀gà Ayẹni, one of the two people with a landline on their street, he would probably send one of his sons to call Ernest.

She sobbed through the call, telling Ernest of how difficult things had been in Barbados before she finally got her visa, of the journey here, and of how confusing she found most things. She told him of her discouragement, and questioned if they were doing the right thing. Ernest remained positive and assured her they were. He reminded her why they were doing this, of how proud of her he was, and of the children's excitement that Mummy was in London. She heard a double beep and looked around the box to see where the sound was coming from. By the time she put the ear piece back, Ernest's voice was gone from the other end. The five-pound credit had run out.

She walked home with a mix of elation and melancholy. Elation at having spoken to her husband, and melancholy at the guilt she felt for leaving her children behind.

Transport in Àkúrẹ́ was mostly limited to their Ìjàpá, with the occasional ọ̀kadà thrown in if Grace didn't tell Ernest.

Ernest hated her taking the ọ̀kadà, ever since he'd seen a terrible accident one afternoon. A pregnant lady had been on the back with two children, and the motorcyclist in his haste to overtake a rather large bus had spilled them all into the gutter. With mud dripping off him, the motorcyclist got out and started screaming back at the market people who were screaming at him for trying to kill all these people. Witnessing the ignorant defiance of the motorcyclist had made Ernest swear never to allow Grace or his children to take the ọ̀kadà again.

In London, Grace found travel puzzling because it was organised. She felt like she was supposed to understand the maze that was the colour-coded bus system. She was more used to the landmark way of finding things back in Àkúrẹ́. Grace smiled as she thought of the old landmarks: the huge mosque at the centre of town, the Ọba's palace, old garage, the catholic cathedral that signalled the end of the buzzing Ọba Adéṣidà road market. A seemingly foolish system to the untrained observer but when you tell a driver to take you to the market near the mosque not the one by the central palace, you were sure to end up in the right place.

Even more puzzling was the tube, so Grace bought a notebook and kept detailed notes on how to get to certain hospitals using whichever form of transport was most appropriate. She also took notes on the landmarks. Her London landmarks were references to distinct types of architecture.

The pace of the city confounded her. Everyone was in a hurry. She dubbed it 'the London pace'. She longed for the meandering pace of Àkúré and the ease of being able to ask anyone for directions. After a few weeks, she joined the march, finding it necessary to stave off the cold November snap.

On top of the transport system was the 4 o'clock sundown hour. She found it hard to get used to, having had it drummed into her as a child that nothing good ever happened after 7 p.m. So all the kids in their neighbourhood headed home for dinner after sundown, but in the new clime she found herself, if she wanted to find a job, she knew she couldn't just head home when it got dark.

On Mondays, she bought a nursing magazine to look at that week's job adverts.

None of her early efforts led to work. That was for first few weeks; the weeks before she met Didi.

———

Grace was standing at the bus stop after yet another rejection from a hospital, this time at Ealing Broadway, when she saw Didi approaching wearing a uniform. Something about Didi made her stop. Maybe it was because Didi's gait reminded her of someone she used to know, or that Grace felt she had a sweet disposition. Later, when looking back on the meeting, Grace was unable to say if she'd ever again be able to muster the courage that carried her forward that day. Still, on that day, she'd approached Didi and asked how she had got her job.

Didi had a sweetness about her when she spoke. She wore glasses, the ends of which disappeared into her long thin dreadlocks, and she had a toothy smile that made Grace think, how did all her teeth fit in her mouth.

"You know our African qualifications are not recognised here, my sister. You have to apply for healthcare assistant roles or as helper in nursing homes first, then, from there, you may be able to cross over to nursing," Didi said.

By the following week, Grace found a job in a nursing home.

———

Ernest had been taking the kids to school by a market bus, which market traders took to the rural farms in the morning. In the absence of an organised public-school bus system and with the taxi being too expensive, he had no choice. Sometimes it meant the kids would be late because the conductor waited for the bus to fill up before moving. Sometimes, a motivated commuter would pay for all the empty seats so they could get going.

On this particular morning there wasn't much room. The greedy conductor had taken advantage of a particularly thin woman in the middle row, and had proceeded to shove five people there. Ìní was upset at the squeeze and hung on to Ernest the whole time. After dropping them off, Ernest went to see their neighbour, Ṣọ̀gà, to see if he would be willing to start taking Démì and Ìní to school along with his own children.

Ṣọ̀gà worked for a commissioner at the Ministry of Transport. He didn't have an official title, and, at least as far as Ernest could tell, he was a general dogsbody for the commissioner. Working at the Ministry of Transport meant that Ṣọ̀gà had access to a fleet of cars; his current car was a jeep, so Ernest knew there was plenty of room to accommodate all five kids.

"Good morning, sir," Ernest greeted Ṣọ̀gà at the door. Ṣọ̀gà was wearing only a white towel with half his face covered in white paste from shaving.

"Well done Ernest, come in. Have you come to use the phone?"

"No sir. I have come on a small matter of my children."

"Hope nothing is wrong?"

"All is well. I just wanted to ask if you could please help drop them in school along with your children in the mornings?"

"Yinka and I were wondering what had happened to your car. We saw you on an ọ̀kadà the other day and we felt sorry. I mean your wife is in the UK. You should be able to afford a car now."

Ernest felt the full force of his jibe but he chose not to rise to the bait. He needed his help. "Money is hard to come by even in UK, sir," he laughed to show he wasn't bothered by the insult.

"Yes, we can help you. As long as you remember us when you start making money at this UK thing."

Ernest thanked him but left slightly annoyed. *Does this moron think we are pushing drugs?*

Ernest entered Alhaji E.O.D.'s office with some trepidation that afternoon. Grace had written to him agreeing it was time to confront the Alhaji as he hadn't paid the final instalment. It had been over three months since Alhaji E.O.D. took over the bookstore. Their main source of income was now gone, the state contracts were not coming through, and Ernest was worried about what to feed the children when they came home from school.

As Ernest entered the store, he saw Alhaji E.O.D.'s first son, the ex-con, smoking ganja outside the store. Leaning against the metal security gates, he didn't acknowledge Ernest's greeting.

As Ernest entered the second set of inner sliding doors, Alhaji E.O.D. popped his head out and greeted him loudly, "Assalam Alaykun, my friend! Come in, long time no see."

The nerve of this man, Ernest thought, but tried to remain calm. "Hello, Alhaji, you know why I'm here."

"Please let's step into my office, so we don't talk in front of these little people." He swept his arm widely to indicate his staff; two of his wives were also there.

"Alhaji, I cannot lie to you. My children are hungry," Ernest said after they had sat down in Alhaji's office. "I don't know where our next meal is coming from and you refuse to pay your next instalment."

"You have to depend on Allah, my—"

"You're NOT even Muslim!"

Ignoring the accusation, Alhaji E.O.D. continued, "My brother, let us stay calm. My children are also hungry, in fact they are entering starvation as we speak. It is not that I refuse to pay my friend, there is no money."

"Then why did you buy the bookshop? If I still had the shop, I could still feed my children with the little sales I was making, one biro here, one eraser there."

"But you would not have been able to pay for your wife's visa," Alhaji said with cruel candour. Seeing Ernest's angry look, he changed tack, "The truth is, we now sell directly to schools, not to parents. So, it is the school that is owing me, and now we have a corrupt principal."

"How many corrupt principals do you have? There are many schools in this area."

Alhaji E.O.D. adjusted his embroidered kufi hat and looked to his left. He was about to lie, and he personally believed Allah was on his right.

"Look, my friend, they are all corrupt. We have been deceived. They are happy to sign the contract and take the books, but when the time is right to pay up, they don't."

Realising the irony and exasperated with the pointless conversational ping-pong, Ernest leaned forward but the Alhaji interrupted him before he could talk.

"My friend, but your wife is abroad…"

"My wife is abroad," Ernest repeated, not sure what to do with the Alhaji's statement. "Money doesn't grow on trees abroad! They work even harder than we do here. My wife has only just started working, she earns a pittance, and after tax there's virtually nothing left."

"My friend, I will advise you to borrow some money and start rearing chickens."

Ernest did his characteristic shoulder tilt to stop himself from lashing out at the Alhaji.

At this, the Alhaji was encouraged, and expatiated further, "If you borrow some money, you may be able to purchase some chickens in addition to the one I gave you before, keep them at home for your children. This is what we have done. On good days when they lay eggs, that is protein for your children, on bad days, you can kill one. But…"

He paused briefly to look at Ernest's reaction then continued, "But try not to kill them, let them multiply first then you can kill and eat one, maybe for Christmas. If you want your children to eat, you can also start growing things. If you come by, Mama Mutia, I think you know my first wife, she can give you some potatoes and tomatoes to grow in your garden. Inshallah, when the school principals have stopped their corruption, I can pay you back," he said, still looking to the left.

Speechless, Ernest looked at his feet and rubbed his neck and head, it was covered in angry sweat. His right leg shook with annoyance. He needed his mind to utter, splutter something, something that could convey his momentary anger and all the other thoughts flooding his brain, but his mind remained vacant. Finally, after the noise in his mind came to a stop, he looked up. Alhaji E.O.D. looked back at him, desperate, and in the moment, all the bravado and the joking seemed to drain from the Alhaji's face, Ernest saw the man behind the mask. He was simply Sam Okoro, a desperate father, also trying to provide for his family.

Ernest had to admit, the Alhaji had a good point. With some of the fruit already growing in their backyard, he was already doing what Alhaji suggested.

When he left Alhaji E.O.D.'s office he started to think. With his rage subsiding and his head clearing, he suddenly had a thought: why should he expect a bookstore that wasn't selling before to suddenly be prosperous? The thought saddened him. It was his dream, and now there was an ever-expanding hole in it. Not to mention he had lost the connection that bookstore gave him with his children, Ìní with her head permanently buried in a book, and Démì, who enjoyed the simple pleasure of being with his father.

Ernest brought home a hen and a rooster one Saturday afternoon in February. Démì and Ìní were ecstatic when they saw them. Chicken was usually for Christmas so it must mean they were celebrating something. Ernest explained to them that it was a new project, and that they would be trying, as a family, to raise their own chicken.

"Now we can have eggs for breakfast when the chicken lays, and when the eggs hatch, we will have more chicken," Ernest explained.

"But how will the eggs hatch if we eat them?" Ìní asked.

"We won't have eaten the ones that hatch," Ernest said, laughing.

Ernest also planted some sweet potatoes, explaining that they were perennial, and that, even after harvest, they would not need to replant because they would grow again in season. The children also helped him as he planted some tomatoes, chilli, and garden eggs.

Ìní felt comforted by the thought of the sweet potatoes growing year after year. *Then we won't ever run out of food*, she thought brightly, aware that sometimes Daddy had to intensely improvise to keep her and Démì's stomachs full.

"Auntie Grace?"

"Yes, come in," said Grace.

"Na me Sylvia. Abeg, you fit watch dem pikin while I go market *quick* quick?"

"No problem, Sylvia. Where is Tómi?"

"Oga don go out. She say she go come back week after next."

"Did she go with Fẹmi?" Grace wondered why Tómi would go away for so long without mentioning it.

"No, Oga dey France."

"Ok, I'll look after the twins. When are you coming back?"

"One hour."

Over the next two weeks, while Tómi and Fẹmi were away from the mansion, Grace helped to look after the twins; mostly after school and at the weekends, when Sylvia had other errands to run.

Grace had started to notice that Tómi and Fẹmi disappeared a lot, especially during term-time. They went separately and without explanation, and would come back during half-term or holidays.

Tomi's disappearances were a mystery. Grace's best guess was some kind of spa, because Tómi always came back with glowing skin and a new wig, which she would hang up along the others. Grace did briefly consider if Tómi was having an affair, but she quickly discarded it – Tómi was too serious, too tightly wound.

Fẹmi, on the other hand, definitely had a mistress or two. The tell-tale signs were there – he was jumpy, and he took all his calls into his study. Even the ones from his 'mother'.

Grace couldn't be sure, but she suspected Tóbi was wise to his father's extramarital affairs. He had dropped some insulated insults lately, which was surprising for someone his age – she suspected he'd heard them from Tómi. To temper the drama, Grace never asked him of his intended meaning.

———

Tómi's brother came to stay. It seemed his visit was unwelcome, as everybody treated him as such, until the circumstances that led to his departure. He also managed to shed light on some of the bizarre behaviour of Fẹ́mi and Tómi.

"You know he's having an affair?" Túndé said unprompted one day at dinner.

"Who? Could you pass the salt please?" Grace asked irritably having asked him twice already.

But Túndé would not be dissuaded. Grace already annoyed him when she interrupted him mid-flow on his thoughts on the upcoming Nigerian elections to ask for the salt. "Ok, play dumb. FẸ́MI IS HAVING AN AFFAIR."

Grace's peripheral vision caught Sylvia backing out of the dining room. "Please don't raise your voice. This thing is not my business," said Grace.

"Fẹ́mi has a girlfriend in France, she's this small Togolese girl, very thin, like this." Túndé waved his fork to indicate how thin she was, then he reached for another drumstick. "I've seen her at one of their homes, pretending to be the househelp. Plus, Tómi is never around, they're terrible parents."

"Aren't your kids also unattended in Nigeria? I hardly think you're one to judge," said Grace.

Having finished eating the drumstick, he reached for two bags of chin-chin piled on a tray in the middle of the dining table. "It's different, I'm not rich." After prolonged chewing of the hard snack, he added, "If you have money, it's no way to parent."

Baffled by his logic and food choices, Grace nodded.

———

It was still very cold so Tómi gave Grace some of her old jumpers to wear.

"Take these and get Sylvia to wash them for you. If you take a bus or tube across town you can get some more winter clothes at Liverpool Street market. It's in East London."

Grace nodded. She did not want to bother Tómi with the minor details of not knowing which was East or West London.

Catching her confused look, Tómi said, "Take Túndé with you, he's idle."

At Kensington High Street station, as Grace popped in her ticket at the turnstile, Túndé pushed in front of her and rolled in. Grace looked up, surprised. Numerous questions swirled round her head, but he stood on the other side grinning. She mouthed some curse words but nothing audible came out. She tried jiggling the turnstiles but they had locked. She could now hear the person behind her smacking their lips in annoyance at having Grace hold up the line with no ticket. So, she went back and bought another.

Túndé, when she confronted him, made some convoluted excuse about needing more money than Grace, and that since she was still in Tómi's good graces it was easier for her to get more. Grace tried to explain that her husband had sold his business to make it possible for her to travel and the little cash she had was not handouts from Tómi. It was like talking to a brick, Túndé remained resolute that his luck was down and it was up to everybody to bring it back up.

At the market, someone tapped Grace on the shoulder as she haggled for a red jumper.

"Grace?"

Grace turned around, it was her old friend Lànà from nursing school, "Lànà!!!!" Arms spread wide, they embraced, "How are you? How is your husband? And the children?" Grace asked.

"We are fine. We are all here, the children moved here two years ago. So, you too are also in England, that our country, nobody is staying! When did you get here?"

"Ah, a few months ago o. Ernest and the kids are also back home."

"What are you doing here?"

"Nursing. I am working as a healthcare assistant but I am trying to find work as a nurse," Grace said.

"Have you done your adaptation?" Lànà asked, stretching out her hand to feel the jumper Grace was trying to buy. At this pause, Túndé cleared his throat to announce his presence.

"Oh, this is my cousin, Túndé. What is adaptation?"

"Good afternoon sir, thank you for taking care of my good friend. God bless you." Turning back to Grace, she said, "You have to do adaptation to convert to a UK-registered nurse."

"Ooooooh oooooh, I think that is why I have been having trouble finding nursing work. Where can I do that now? How much is it?" Grace said.

"It is three hundred pounds, there is a hospital in West London where you... here hold this," handing Túndé and Grace a shopping bag each, she reached into her handbag, rummaged for a little bit, then pulled out a torn piece of paper and biro. As she wrote, she said, "This is where you can do your adaptation, go and see them on Monday and you can get the information pack. Here is my number and our address. In fact, come by next weekend. I hope the kids will still remember you," said Lànà.

———

Grace borrowed the money for the conversion course from Tómi. It would be six-months of work experience at a hospital, and afterwards she could be a full-fledged nurse.

On the eve of her interview she looked for her passport, but to no avail. Failing to find it, she went for the interview and promised to bring it later. Her fortunes turned at the interview and she got the adaptation role, but the passport remained missing. She had two weeks to find it before the job began.

She told Tómi about the missing passport, but Tómi seemed nonchalant. It was hard for Grace to decipher if Tómi was just being callous or she didn't really understand the gravity of the missing passport. She asked Tómi again a few days later, at which point Tómi called Sylvia on the intercom and instructed her to ask all the staff to help look for Grace's passport.

A day before Grace was due to start the conversion course, and with the passport still missing, she overheard a conversation between Sylvia and one of the security guards. As they saw her approaching, they scuttled away. It was clear the conversation was about her. One word she caught stood out to her, *oríolórí*. Grace mulled over the meaning in her mind – it literally translated as *someone else's head*. It didn't mean anything she recognised. Then she thought back to her conversation where Sylvia said she didn't speak Yorùbá, so how come she was throwing around words like *oríolórí?*

Later that evening, Ernest called her on the house phone and she vented about the missing passport, Tómi's cavalier attitude, and the overheard conversation. She was now nervous she would lose the adaptation job. Ernest asked to speak with Fẹ́mi, so she went to look for him.

She stood outside Fẹ́mi's study, but couldn't glean what the conversation was about exactly. Fẹ́mi could be quiet when it suited him: his glory days as a politico had taught him the less he said, the less he'd have to defend later.

Later Fẹ́mi came out of his study, saw Grace standing outside and curtly said, "We will search Túndé's things," and with that, he headed down the corridor and Grace followed him. When he reached Túndé's room, she stood outside while he went in.

A loud argument in Yorùbá ensued with threats from Túndé about Fẹ́mi's mysterious past as a politician. After several more curses, Fẹ́mi walked out with multiple passports, including Grace's. By the end of that week, Túndé was gone.

There was no explanation offered, and she didn't ask.

Shortly after that, Grace moved out to Brixton.

"Oya come," said Ernest. It was Ìní's turn. He put Démì down and carried Ìní on his back.

They kept walking. He looked at his watch, they had been walking for forty-five minutes. They were now at the top of the road leading from the government quarters to the roundabout to turn towards Dr Òshénì's house.

He stopped to look behind him. Démì had stopped to vomit again.

Then Ìní started groaning behind him. "Daddy, I need to go," she barely made it to the gutter before she spewed out the contents of her stomach.

Kí là won ọmọ yìí jẹ? Ernest ran through his mind. They'd had Golden Morn for breakfast. He'd added some evaporated milk to Ìní's but not to Démì's – he didn't like it. *Maybe it was the evaporated milk? Had it gone off?* But Ernest had had some too and he had been fine.

Then for lunch, his sister Yẹyè had come over to cook and watch them while Ernest went to the governor's house to collect his cheque.

What did she feed them? The kids had said rice and stew. Nothing strange there. They had that all the time. I shouldn't have gone to that meeting. It was pointless anyway and I didn't manage to get my cheque.

He looked over. Ìní was now kneeling with her hands clutched over the edge of the gutter. Her eyes bulging as she retched for her life. Démì stood worried looking at her, having managed to spill his guts in a more dignified manner. He wiped his mouth on the edge of his top.

The place now stunk with the glorious steam of the vomit.

Ìní, exhausted, was now sitting on the side of the road.

Ernest approached and examined the vomit to see what had made them sick. The streetlights were dim despite it being a government area, all he could make out were undigested bits of rice and lots of other white stuff.

No matter. They must continue. They had another fifteen minutes to go.

"We're almost there, sweethearts. Shall we continue?"

Démì turned to retch again. This time, it was with the same ferocity as Ìní's vomit.

Ernest sat on the floor with Ìní and held her. She had started to cry. Silent tears of fear flowed down his own cheeks.

"*What if they didn't make it to the doctor on time?*"

"What had these kids eaten?"

"What if his sister had accidentally poisoned them?"

Yẹyè lived in a poor area and there was no one with a landline on her street, otherwise he would call her.

He felt crazy with fear.

He wondered what Grace would do.

A taxi with blinding headlights rode past and he wished he had money so they could take a taxi the rest of the way.

Now calm, he asked the kids if they were ok to continue. They were, so they did.

As they left the government area, it got even darker – there were no streetlights and very few cars. It was now sundown so they struggled to see but his children trudged on. He was proud of them. The vomits now infrequent, and mostly retching instead of stomach contents coming out.

The doctor's place was a huge house in a neighbourhood that was slowly being built up, so the houses were few and far between. Most of the area was mid-construction and there were empty plots of land everywhere, separated with high fences with serrated wires and broken bottles cemented on top. From the wrong angle, it looked like a prison precinct.

The doctor was a distant cousin of Grace's so they were seen immediately. He was making small talk about having just come back from the office and wasn't Ernest in luck to have found him at home.

When the doctor started to examine the children, Ernest sat in his chair and cried silently.

Dr Òshénì came out and knew Ernest had been crying.

"Ernest, it's ok now. They just ate something bad. They'll be fine. I've given them some anti-emetics. Although I don't think they need it, most of their stomach is empty."

"Ah…" Ernest was exhausted and couldn't make out any words. He felt guilt tremors running down his back and through to his toes.

"Pẹ̀lẹ́, Ernest. My own children are the same. They eat from the garden all the time and I tell them to ask me before they eat anything."

"They ate from the garden? Is that what they told you?" Ernest said alarmed.

"Yes, they said they ate some fruits from the garden when you were not home and your sister, I believe, went out briefly to meet some man that came to the house," Dr Òshénì said.

Ernest clutched his head in despair, his shoulders shaking as he wept again. Unsure what to do, Dr Òshénì came and stood by, patting him on the shoulder intermittently.

By way of consoling him, Dr Òshénì offered for his driver to drop them off at home.

Démì's memory of that night mostly constituted of his father carrying him and his sister on his back interchangeably, as they walked for an hour to the doctor's house. Years later when retelling the story Démì would say, "That night I knew my father was superman."

For weeks after the incident, Ernest watched both his children like a hawk. He rarely left the house in the evenings after they came back from school. It took months for him to fully relax and when he eventually mentioned the event to Grace, it became a footnote rather than the entire chapter that it had been to him.

After that, he resolved to get a car by all means, figuring he would have long been back home that afternoon before they had eaten the poison, or perhaps he could have got them to the doctor faster. Whichever way he looked at the incident, for years he blamed himself.

———

On a particularly blistering afternoon, Ernest stopped by his post-office box. His stomach flipped a little as he reached in his pocket for his keys. It was Friday. New mail day. Maybe Grace had written.

He picked out the letters slowly, there was an unfamiliar one with the government stamp. No letter from Grace.

"Hey, my friend!"

Ernest looked up to find someone standing in front of him, staring him down. Ernest was tall, not a lot of people stared down at him. It was Cornelius, he owned a plastics store on Àràkálẹ̀ road.

"Ah, my friend. Corne-stical! How are you? How is the shop?"

"Ernest, Je-re-ma-yah! God is in control. It is your face I'm seeing like this. How is Madam?"

"She is good, we thank God. I just went to see if we had any letters from her," Ernest said.

"Eviction notice? What is that?" Cornelius pointed to what Ernest was holding. Ernest did not realise it was stamped on the outside of the brown envelope he was holding so plainly. Cornelius could see the big blue letters clearly from his vantage point.

"Where?" Ernest flipped through the letters. It was the unfamiliar letter, and Cornelius was right, on the top right-hand corner was the solid blue writing: GOVERNMENT QUARTERS – EVICTION NOTICE.

Chapter 4

My darling Gracious,

Words cannot express how much I miss your beautiful face and your beautiful smile. Your children miss you very much.

Yesterday, I was playing the record of that musician that you like on the radiogram – Comfort Omoge – what a sonorous voice! It reminded me of when we first became friends and we would attend discos at your friend's house. I miss our conversations in the kitchen, hiding from everyone so we could catch up on the latest records. It was during those chats that I fell in love with you. Your beautiful smile, your big open heart. The way you listen so carefully and remember the little details that I say and what I don't say.

I miss the way you are always looking for something to do with your hands to keep busy, the way you are always helping out your friends and no job is too small for you to do. You did and still inspire me every day...

Last week, we moved into the two rooms above the church which Pastor Kolawole gave us. I think I told you on the phone the Ministry wrote to us and said you were no longer in employment with them and that we must move.

The rooms are very comfortable, although we have to be out Thursday evenings because they use the rooms for prayer for the women's ministry. I have enrolled the children in after-school lessons on Thursday so we have somewhere to go – Ini takes extra classes with her English teacher and Demi takes extra Maths plus

English. The children love the extra tuition and they miss you very much.

Demi will go to secondary school next year, we have already started applying for places that have boarding schools so he can focus on his studies.

I hope your work is going well. Stay encouraged because even though we miss you here, your going is for a purpose and that purpose shall be achieved. We are already seeing results because the children can stay in school and Ini has caught up and is very happy.

Meeting you is still the most fortunate thing that ever happened to me and I will be forever grateful. Hurry back so our family can reunite.

Still in love,

Ernest

Démì had taken to hiding in his room after school.

One day Ernest walked in and found him on the floor.

"Why are you reading on the floor, Démì? What's wrong with your bed?"

Silence.

Démì looked at the bed and said nothing.

"Is something wrong with your bed?"

Silence.

"Why don't you answer me?"

Ernest lifted the cover and saw that Démì had piled his clothes on the bed near the centre and under it was a round imprint of pee. The patch was so huge that as soon as it got some air, it started to smell.

"We have to wash this," Ernest said. "Why didn't you tell me?"

"I didn't want you to be disappointed in me. I didn't used to wet the bed."

"Use to," Ernest corrected.

"I didn't use to wet the bed," Démì repeated.

"You should have told me. This is not hygienic. I don't want you to get sick. Your mother will kill me. Oya come, let's take this downstairs to go and soak it."

Démì followed his father through the narrow hallway of the church and then downstairs into the kitchen, where he got a plastic bowl, poured some *Omo* detergent in it and soaked all his shirts and trousers that had been marinating in urine.

Démì waited to be told off by Ernest, it didn't come. In that moment, he'd never loved his father more, although he didn't know how to express it so he kept silent.

Ernest felt guilty. He knew the upheaval was hard on the kids and it wasn't lost on him that on Wednesday nights before they had to move all their stuff out for the women's prayers, Ìní always had nightmares and would scream most of the night.

They had to move, he vowed within himself.

Ìní was crying again. It was breaking his heart. Ernest tried another tactic – combing from the back. She had been rubbing her head on something, there were extra knots on the back. He breathed slowly as he ran the comb through her tight black curls.

They hadn't brushed it yesterday because Ìní had got upset and ran away. "Mummy lets me do my own hair!"

Rather than chase her, he let her run. Ernest, conscious of school-gate gossip and people saying *these children were neater when their mother was around*, always made sure that their uniforms were washed twice-weekly and carefully pressed, their white shirts shining with no tell-tale stains, that Démì's hair was neat and brushed carefully until the pomade glistened between the nestled curls, and that Ìní's hair was sleeked and packed into a single afro cloud.

Démì wandered in, shoes in hand. "Daddy, I need you to do my shoes."

"Démì, you know how to do your own shoes now."

"Daddy, but these ones have *okun.*"

"They're called laces, Démì. Let me finish your sister's hair and then I will help you."

Ernest was taking them on an outing. The kids always got excited whenever Ernest announced an outing. They'd not had one since Ernest sold the car. Today, he'd borrowed Simon's car, and had some extra money from a contract that had just paid out.

Ernest bent over to tie Démì's shoes, realising they were getting tight, and that they would need to think about getting new ones soon. He grabbed his keys and they left.

In the car, the kids sang the '*Dòdò àti Rice*' song. Démì drummed the dashboard along in rhythm; Ernest had no idea Démì could drum.

Ernest had a few errands to run. First, they went to the bank to cash his cheque. Then he took them to Simon's shop, where he and Simon discussed some business matters while the kids hung out on the front porch of the shop, counting all the blue cars that went by. Later, Ernest could see them through the window of Simon's office playing with the children of the lady who owned the shop next door.

After about half an hour, he called on them to leave, and they went to the barber's. He wondered if he should have warned Ìní that she was getting a haircut too.

"What style do you want?" the barber asked.

Surprised, Ìní looked at Ernest. He got up from his seat and pointed to a poster on a wall full of haircut ideas.

"Ìní, you can pick any haircut that you want from the poster, or you can also go for something like your brother's – short and neat."

Ìní pointed to Démì's haircut and sat silently while the barber buzzed her hair to look the same.

———

After the oríolórí episode, Grace got a second job and moved into a flatshare above a hairdressing shop in Brixton. It was run by a gentlemanly Indian man from Kenya and was close to a bus stop.

The rent was half of her wages from both jobs but she was happy that she no longer had to put up with the bedlam in Tómi's house.

The room had a bed and a small table by the wall and nothing else. She kept her clothes in a suitcase on the floor, and her shoes piled under the table. The heating panel had fallen from its hinges and did not work.

On the first night, she couldn't sleep from itching so much and she was cold, so she stripped the sheets and unzipped the mattress cover to discover an eclipse of moths. Figuring they'd been there long before her and it was therefore their rightful home, she left it for them and took to sleeping in the living room. Anyway, it was warmer in the living room, it being the only room in the house with any form of heating.

———

The nightcrawlers in Brixton were much like the ones in Ìsàlẹ̀ Èkó bridge in Lagos: drug-addicted prostitutes and area boys. Walking home after a night shift was terrifying, so Grace developed an aggressive gait and an even scarier attitude. She muttered loudly to herself to deter anyone trying to approach her. On nights when her aggressive stagger didn't work, she would supplement it with jerky head movements to give an illusion that she herself was a nightcrawler.

Her focus was her children and it kept her going. She wanted to build a better life and education for them. They couldn't do that if she was stuck in Àkúrẹ́ with no money to send them to school.

On nights when her knees were aching from standing all day and all evening at her second job, when she was close to giving up, it was the goal of educating her children that kept her focused. She had finally started sending money home, first for the basics, and then they would start saving for a car.

Grace developed an innate deafness to tricky situations; she dealt with things by saying nothing. This completely mystified her colleagues who found solidarity in complaining. Grace saw it as a waste of time and would rather get on with things. She was a great listener, a sanctuary of silence in which they found comfort. No one could find her edges.

As a junior healthcare assistant, she got the worst shifts, but she did not mind as long as she had work. But to Ernest, she bared her tired soul and her body aches, her emotional sprains and strains, and the pain hiding in her secret places.

Sometimes, she'd write letters to Ernest, writing of Démì, and of how much she missed his analytical mind, and of Ìní, with her incredible memory of mundane but poignant childhood moments. She kept the letters in a heap by the door until she could afford to mail them.

———

"Hello, HELLO????"

"Hello, can I speak to Ernest please?"

"Who?"

"Ernest," Grace said. After a short silence followed by some static noise, she repeated, "Can I speak to my husband, Ernest please?"

She could hear a voice muttering in the background in Yorùbá, "Àwọn wo le lé yìí báyìí. Mo ti ní kán yé pe bí yìí." Then more clearly a man's voice, "Hello, who is this? There is no Ernest here."

Figuring the line had been crossed again, she hung up and dialled anew. This time she got through to Ṣọ̀gà's house – she recognised the sing-song Òndó lilt in his accent. She didn't get around to asking for Ernest; they couldn't hear her, but she could hear them. After several tries, her credit ran out, and she could hear the disappointing long beep of the dial tone. Dejected, Grace hung up and went home.

———

"How can you do it? You said you have small children back home?" Kinsi said. Kinsi was Grace's colleague. She had big eyes and a small mouth and talked constantly. Today, it was about the state of Grace's family split across two continents.

Kinsi had not been the first to ask her this question. It wasn't that she didn't want to answer, but the answer was caught in the quagmire of her mind. Even if she could unravel it, to articulate it was another matter.

How could she speak of the fears that spurred her on, yet at other times woke her with nightmares? How could she speak of the illiteracy that threatened to doom her children to a life without dreams or choices? She'd watched Ernest give up his dream of owning a bookstore, despite all his best efforts.

She longed for the Ernest of the old years when he had just started the bookstore, she longed for the gleam in his eye when he talked of how his hobby and work had merged into one.

It still puzzled, yet gratified her, as to how Mama, in her quiet but cunning way, had pushed for her to be educated even when it was unpopular to educate a girl.

How could she speak of all this when all she heard in the hallways were rumblings of how the weekends weren't long enough? How could she speak of all this when all she wanted was to get back to work, so hard-pressed between her loneliness and lack of means that sometimes work became her only solace? How could she speak of all this when all she heard from colleagues was how much they had spent on nonessentials like decorating or holidays, watching them eat sandwiches from the canteen at a price that she knew could feed her family for a week?

So, she answered in the same way she had the others. She lied.

"You just do. It's not so bad," Grace said with a half-smile. "Also, you get paid for the work that you do, back home in my country, you could work for months and not see a penny."

"But you have another job after this? Gary told me," Kinsi added, referring to the head nurse in the ward.

"Yes," Grace said without further explanation.

Kinsi observed Grace quietly. She knew better than to wait for anything further.

———

"So, I heard oríolórí. I told Ernest and he spoke with Fẹ́mi, the next thing I know, Fẹ́mi went into Túndé's room and came out with all these passports, including mine," Grace spread her arms out in wonder, as she told Lànà the bizarre tale of her missing passport.

"Oríolórí is the black-market for passport selling o," Lànà replied, her eyebrows almost touching her hairline in amazement. "I've heard of it but never seen it, these people steal passports with a visa in it for money. Did you ask Túndé why he took your passport?"

"You know me... I hate conflict. It feels rough on my skin. Also, he was gone shortly after that. Me, I didn't ask o. I was just glad when he left."

"So where are you now living?"

"In this two-bedroom flatshare in Brixton. It costs half my two salaries, there's no heating, and there are moths in the mattress so I sleep on the sofa. But it is close to the bus stops," Grace said.

"You have to move out. You must! You can stay with my cousin, Auntie BB, in Peckham. In fact, she is coming by here later tonight, I will ask her for you."

That evening, in between reminiscing about old times, the old friends connected on a new level – that peculiar coin-in-a-tin feeling of rattling around alone in a foreign country.

"Half of my mind is blank half of the time, they call me hardworking, I just laugh. You know when it's just you, you think about so many things..."

"It's like your head is full of this whooooo sound," Lànà expanded her hands in an empty hug. "But there is no sound per se... like a loud silence, you know when a patient has tinnitus but without the noise *sha*," she concluded, having found her place in the jumble of gestures and words. She rested both hands in her lap, exhausted by the explanation.

"There is no one to share anything with so your conversations are all in your own head," Grace agreed.

"Hmmm, I had that my first few weeks here when we first moved," Lànà said. "Most of the time I didn't recognise the road I was on or where I was going. You know, we come from a place with no underground transport. What is tube kẹ̀? So, I would come out of the underground disoriented. How about the first time I used the A to Z to drive to an interview..."

"What is A to Z?" Grace asked.

"It is the map... the map of all the roads in the UK," Lànà said.

"Ah, if only our country would do that." Grace waved her right hand sarcastically.

"Half of my... er I was so empty minded," Lànà gestured to her head. "I was driving Junior once to one of his university open days. Half of my mind was back home, the other half was here, trying to read the A to Z. I had never used it before. God saved us that day, so many near misses."

Grace shared a recurring dream with her friend. "I keep having a dream that I go back home. It doesn't make sense. I can't go back for another few years, not until I have a proper nursing job and my papers. I miss my children." She paused, taken aback by her candour to an old classmate she hadn't seen for about two decades. She let it sit in the air, breathing, between them.

"Don't worry about it," Lànà responded with levity. "That is a common dream. It's even more common when you're about to go back, and that time will come, my friend, it will come."

When she left Lànà's that evening, Grace walked into a cloud so thick it terrified her. She backed away immediately into the house, stepping on Lànà's foot.

Lànà yelped, "What is it?"

"Sorry! But what is this outside? It's hard to see."

Lànà laughed and said, "Don't worry. It's just fog. Keep going." She described in detail how to walk back to the tube stop.

It was the first time Grace would see fog. The experience stayed with her like a meteorological memory of her silent tinnitus. Such that every time she saw fog after that she was reminded of that evening with Lànà, of finally being able to put into words the quagmire of her lonely mind.

The memory was neither joyous nor sad, but it sat under her skin as yet another milestone in her journey. There was no such thing as fog in Nigeria, there were two seasons: summer and harmattan – a slightly dryer, harsher form of summer with cold mornings and even hotter afternoons.

———

My darling Gracious,

I hope you are well. The children are doing very well and send their love to you. I have enclosed a short letter from Demi, he wanted to tell you how Sports Day went. He was in Yellow House and he has made a new friend in his class, Ortega Olorunsogo. He is a nice boy and does not seem spoilt like the other commissioners' and ministers' children.

Last week, Demi and Ini were doing impressions of Soga Ayeni in the house. As it turns out, he is very abusive towards his children, swearing at them in the car in the name of Sango, the god of thunder. I have therefore decided to withdraw them from his care, he will no longer be taking them to school. I have asked Mr Balogun instead – the man with the upstairs house at the end of our road, it is much further but only an extra fifteen-minute walk so I have been taking the children there instead.

All these makes me realise we will need to get a car soon.

How are things at work? How is your boss, Gary?

Still in love with you,

Ernest

Chapter 5

Ernest was heading to Simon's house to discuss problems with their contract to supply army boots for ten thousand soldiers across four barracks in Akwa-Ibom State in the East.

Initially he had been nervous about the project and he had said to Simon, "I've never been to Akwa-Ibom."

"We don't need to go to Akwa-Ibom," Simon assured him. "We just need to pay a supplier for the rubber boots, add our own on top and get a driver to deliver the boots to the barracks."

When he got to Simon's, the gateman let him in and he walked up to the main house. Simon was home alone, his wife was at work and his children were in school.

"So, what did you say the problem was with these boots?" Ernest said taking a sip of Mirinda.

"They are too small, they are made in Nigeria but someone has tagged them 'Made in America' so they have come up small."

"Will we get paid?" Ernest asked worriedly. He was thinking he'd be happy to walk away with no money, given the error and the fact that it was his first project and he was lucky to get it. Although he had been counting on the money for school fees.

"Ah ah, why not? I know some things about that governor. Don't worry, our money will come out! Come rain or shine!" Simon beat his right hand on his chest for emphasis.

Ernest did not ask why he was so sure.

When Grace had first met Simon, she had despised him because of his shady dealings and she privately called him Simon Máwobẹ̀ (Simon, don't look there) because if Simon told you to look at something, it was because he wanted to distract you for long enough to rob you blind. Still he was Ernest's friend and seeing Ernest's eternal devotion and gratitude to Simon, she knew it was hopeless saying anything and she always tried to respect him. Until one day, she had sarcastically muttered "Simon Máwobẹ̀" in response to something Ernest had said. Too late to deny it, it was out there. She paused briefly, trying not to laugh and then explained that she had never really trusted Simon. Taken aback by the revelation, Ernest had also revealed he didn't trust Simon that far either but the guy had done too much for him, for him to now turn his back.

These were the thoughts in Ernest's mind when he was thinking how they were going to collect their money on the failed Akwa-Ibom boot supply. It was quite absurd to expect payment, they looked like children's shoes and nobody would wear them.

But the elected official for government contracting for that state was also corrupt and didn't check the boots, and that was how he came to issue their cheque. Turned out he had his own to collect, Simon had promised him a cut if he gave them the out-of-state contract.

Ernest drove them back from Akwa-Ibom, on the way, he planned what he would buy his kids for supper. *Plantain, that was a luxury. They hadn't had plantain since Grace left. Yes, they would have plantain. Yam too.* Even with his superior haggling skills, he hadn't been able to make the delectable tubers affordable for months.

Whistling as he drove, Ernest dreamed of a better immediate future.

Simon, hated when his friend whistled like this, but he realised a small miracle had just happened, so he kept quiet, unwilling to ruin his sweet friend's good mood.

Ernest sat by the window in the living room of their small apartment. He was watching Ìní play by herself on the other side of the room. The long edge of the trapezium-shaped living room led into a narrow hallway, which formed an awkward L-shaped corner that couldn't be used for much. Undeterred, the kids took advantage of the empty corner and would play there often.

Ernest had bought the children some pre-paid envelopes so they could write to their mother. Démì was keen to tell his mum about his new friend in his French class. Ìní thought it was a good exercise to show off the big words she had been learning.

Ìní, who was now seven, got a section within Ernest's folio and she enthusiastically, although somewhat incoherently wrote about her newly learnt words and how worried she was about the upcoming

Sports Day event because even though she was better at running, they had put her on the egg-and-spoon race, and she kept dropping the egg during the heat practice.

Démì, who was now nine, was deemed old enough for his own folio. He studied the edges, saw the intricate designs of the self-sealing page and how it would eventually neatly fold into an envelope. He turned the sheet over, "Air mail, par avion," he read out loud. He looked up at his father questioningly. Ernest hadn't been listening. He was intent on monitoring Ìní and making sure she was not writing outside the lines.

"Daddy, what does this mean?" Démì said.

"Read it to me again."

"Air mail par avion."

"Par avion is French for 'by air'. England is really far away so our letters will be carried by airplane to Mum."

"Oh wow!" Démì started to fold the folio into a paper plane, to aid the mail man, he reasoned.

"Démì, don't do that. You'll spoil the paper, just write in the blank part within the lines."

Démì spent hours by the window writing his letter. First, he wrote in pencil, then he began to trace it in a blue biro. He wanted to convey everything in the sky-blue pages, careful not to write anything in the glue-ready margins, otherwise it may never be read. Afterwards, Ernest proofread it and told Démì what he could do better.

———

"Daddy, what are you cooking?" Démì stood on his favourite kitchen stool, stretching to see above the oven.

"Adémọlá," using his son's full name and pausing for effect as he searched his mind to come up with a name for his recipe. "This is what I call… Progose melegba."

"Progose, progose, progose!" Démì said in a sing-song voice.

Ìní padded in, barefoot.

"Progose, progose, progose," they both now chorused.

Ernest beamed, he had no idea his made-up recipe of all they had left in the house – some garri and beans fried together – would inspire such ditties. But still he loved to see them laughing like this.

He tasted some, retracting his hand quickly – the pan seared his index finger. Very pleased with the result, he used a spoon to scoop some, blew on it, then proffered it to the kids to taste some.

"Thank you, Daddy," they chorused.

"You're welcome, do you like it? It's a new recipe, your mum doesn't know about it but you can tell her in your next letter."

"Progose, progose, progose makes you grow!" Ernest sang.

"But Dad, you said it is ok that I am small like Mummy," Ìní reasoned.

"Yes, it is true but if you have progose, you can grow even taller than your Mum."

———

"Ìní, come. Who gave you this haircut? You look like a garçon." Aunty Yẹyè was in town running away from the latest quarrel with her husband. She had been around for two weeks and the end of her visit was not in sight. She skulked around the house insulting the children and hiding from Ernest so she wouldn't have to explain what the fight with her husband was about.

"Aunty, what is a garçon?" Démì asked.

"My daughter does not look like a boy o," Ernest answered from the other room.

"Then she should wear earrings. Here…" she took off her own earrings and pushed them into Ìní's empty earlobes turning her around abruptly to put on the butterfly backs. "What happened to your earrings?"

"I lost one," Ìní said looking down.

Démì had never liked Aunty Yẹyè because of her bullish behaviour but he liked that she brought them boiled eggs every time she came to visit.

That evening he whispered to Ìní that they should put pins in her mattress on the living room floor to make her uncomfortable so this time she wouldn't stay so long.

Aunty Yẹyè discovered the pins that night before she slept and suspected the children but she had no proof so she kept quiet.

Ernest, noticing the children disappearing and whispering a lot, finally called his sister and questioned her pointedly on why she was running from her husband. The next day she was gone.

———

Grace moved in with Aunty BB on a Sunday morning in early January. The air was a bitter shade of cold. She had celebrated Christmas alone in her flat in Brixton so she was looking forward to some company. She took two buses from Brixton to the estate in Peckham. She took a tiny tumble as she attempted to drag her suitcases onto the second bus, a pair of hands reached out to help but they failed to catch her and she fell backwards. Her grazed ankle bled through her tights, which she nursed under the bus shelter as she waited fifteen minutes for the next bus.

BB and her husband, Báyọ̀, lived in a small two-bedroom flat on Barberton estate in the heart of Peckham. Their flat was on the eighth floor of a mustard-coloured complex.

BB had moved to London with her older siblings in the early 80s when the immigration laws were a bit more lax. She'd met her husband, Báyọ̀, when they were A-Level students, they'd fallen in love and made London their home.

They had a huge network of friends and relatives from Nigeria, who sometimes passed by and stayed with no end date. Sometimes, they also housed others from Lagos as a favour to people who needed a temporary place to stay. Some of their revolving door friends had nicknamed the estate Babátúndé estate, which coincided with a timely vandalism on the estate sign.

The constant flow of people made their flat the perfect place to meet and connect with people, but for some of the longer-staying residents, it became a constant source of annoyance.

Through BB, Grace found the Nigerian community in Peckham to buy food items that she found more familiar. She also found it cheaper than shopping in supermarkets.

BB hosted a house church twice-weekly, which she presided over and expected everybody to attend.

Grace arrived at the flat to BB's literal open arms. Immediately, she felt at home. BB showed her the room she'd be staying in, it had two bunk beds adjacently arranged in an L-shape, such that the door swung open to hit one of the beds, thus jarring awake the woman asleep in one of them.

"Oh, that is Rọ́lákẹ́. She works nights so she sleeps during the day. Our home is your home. I'm making jollof rice." BB talked as Grace followed her out of the room. "When you have put down your bags, come and join us. My two younger brothers are also staying here, so you will meet them, lovely young Christian boys."

BB stretched down to pick up a used diaper while her soliloquy continued, "My husband, Báyọ̀, is at work. He's a bus driver. He'll be home in the evening. Lànà, my cousin, said you start your new job tomorrow?"

"Yes, ma. Infact, I need to go out now to buy my uniform."

After lunch, Grace headed out. She carried hope in her step, with a new place to live, a new job, and a new hope of an easier home life. But she deeply missed her children. Each time she thought about them, her mind wandered to the precipice of a gaping hole, then she would feel an internal wooden bodice pull her back up and away from the precipice. She would snap back to the present moment figuring it was no use, no use exploring the vacuum and the endlessness. She had a job to do here and every day brought her a few steps closer. She would focus on the daily steps not the journey ahead.

Grace entered the first store on the non-trendy discount-store end of Oxford Street, just as Lànà had told her. The one with the blue front and the makeshift chalk signs. She checked a few sleeves for the price tags, dropping them in shock. It was the price of two days' wages for an entire uniform set. She ended up spending forty pounds, she mentally calculated it could feed an entire family for several weeks back home. Lànà had warned her against the mentality of converting everything to Naira, otherwise she'd never do anything. She now had a hundred pounds left from the pocket money Ernest had given her from the sale of the bookstore. She made a mental note to ask him if Alhaji E.O.D. had paid the final instalment.

———

The next day Grace marched excitedly through the double doors of the hospital, she was starting her first day, she knew this was an important milestone in her journey. Things were looking up. She had several bags with her that morning, one with her paperwork, one containing her lunch and where was the other one? Grace rumbled through the carrier bags, doing a mental countdown. Alas! She had left her uniform on the train.

What was I thinking? Grace's mind raced through a mental list of what had preoccupied her that morning. *Money worries, her children, getting on the right bus, getting off at the right stop, nerves about her first day, tiredness from not sleeping well, then back to her children. In the jumbled highway of her mind, she must have stepped off the bus and left one of her bags.*

She looked ahead at the sliding doors leading into the main ward and felt defeated. But that internal wooden bodice, that always held her up at the times when she was about to fall apart the most, did not disappoint. She leaned into the bodice and marched into reception. She asked for Laura, the senior sister to whom she was to report.

The intuitive receptionist saw the haunted look on her face and tried to reassure her, "Don't worry, Laura is really nice, she hired me too." Grace struggled to understand her accent, eventually she said, "I left my uniform on the train, can you please help me?"

"Oh no, I'm so sorry, don't be upset. We always have spares for the agency staff." Laura came to the reception desk at that point and took Grace with her to show her around.

They gave her spare uniforms that day to tide her over until pay day. The money she had left was for food and she did not want to spend it on another set of uniforms.

After her first pay check, she sent some money to Ernest, the children's school fees were due and Alhaji E.O.D. still hadn't paid the last instalment for the purchase of the bookstore.

Grace had noticed a certain cold front from BB lately but couldn't be sure. That morning, Grace walked through the living room while BB was plaiting someone's hair. Not wanting to intrude, she said a quick hello on her way to the kitchen but BB did not respond. Maybe she didn't hear me, Grace thought.

On her way back from the kitchen, Grace moved closer and said, "Hello, Aunty BB." The person whose hair was being plaited looked up, BB remained silent. Grace walked away and went to work.

Later that day, Grace ran into BB's husband in the hallway.

"How are you, my dear sister?" Báyọ̀ said.

"Uncle Báyọ̀, I'm good o."

"How is work?"

"It's going well. I have six months to complete my conversion course but my boss thinks I can do it in three."

"Oh good, that's good."

"Have you seen Aunty BB?"

"She went to the market, we need some meat for the stew on Saturday. She's throwing a small party.

"Has she said anything about me?"

"No, why?"

"She hasn't really been speaking to me. I think she may be angry or something."

"Well, she said someone took the meat from the jollof rice in the fridge and put the jollof back."

"And she thought it was me?"

"Well the others denied it, so…" he stretched his arms out.

"Uncle, I swear it's not me. It must be all the visitors coming and going in here."

"Don't worry about it, my sister, if someone stole the meat, well every day is for the thief." He pronounced it 'tief'. "My wife can be funny." He shrugged and started walking down the hallway. "She's funny,' he added as he entered his bedroom and closed the door.

BB's small party turned out to be twenty-eight people. Grace tried to make amends on the errant meat, but after BB's further avoidance, she decided to leave it.

A few days later, it was like BB had forgotten and she was speaking to Grace again.

"Aunty Grace," she said one afternoon, "I am going to Nigeria in a few weeks, do you have a letter for Uncle Ernest and your children?"

Figuring the ice had thawed, Grace's gratitude was visible, "Yes, Aunty BB, thank you so much."

Grace ran into Aunty BB pulling a trolley on Salwell road in Camberwell. "Aunty, well done o. What have you been buying?"

"Just some *shickin*. I'm going to make stew." Aunty BB, much like her husband Báyọ̀, had some knowledge gaps in pronunciation such that she mixed up her hard 'ch' sounds with soft 'sh' sounds.

"But why do you need a trolley?" Grace said.

"Because I have bought *shickin* for a month," Aunty BB smiled widely exposing her one dead tooth. "You should buy one of these," she advised and looked down proudly at her trolley. It was covered in blue canvas with two wheels, one of the wheels had flattened slightly on one side such that as she pulled, it made a clack-clack sound every few seconds on the uneven streets. Part of the canvas had slightly collapsed on one side near the middle zip and garri occasionally poured through as she wheeled it along. "When you have your own place, you need to buy a deep freezer too, so you're not shopping often. Then you can put your *shickin*, you could even make moin-moin and freeze it so when you peel and grind the beans, you can do the work all at once and it lasts and lasts," she smiled smugly and nodded.

"Yes, Aunty," said Grace, realising it was good advice.

"Gentlemen, the calabash does not have two eyes," Ambrose Koko said.

Not catching his meaning, the two men looked at each other. After an awkward pause, with the bodyguard by the door shifting from foot to foot, his keys clanking on his straddled gun, Ambrose continued, "Let me be brief. We have restructured our tenderisation process. The governor has reallocated your contract to someone else."

Ambrose had a broad accent and he often used the wrong words, which made him difficult to understand and made Ernest wonder how he got such a high office in government. He pronounced English words in a phonetic Igbo accent and to confound the matter further, he would occasionally switch into a high-gear American accent.

"Tenderisation process?" Simon asked, confused.

"We are not at tender stage anymore," Ernest added helpfully. "We already signed an agreement with you and we have secured a lease for the building where we are going to store the cocoa."

"Yes, we've got a five-year lease," Simon added.

"What can I say, the governor has sold it," said Ambrose.

"We will sue," said Simon getting up.

"Sue who? And where? In which court?" Ambrose started laughing and his bodyguard joined in.

"Mr Koko, I beg you if there is anything you can do for us. We have borrowed money to be able to complete this contract, please sir," Ernest said.

Ambrose adjusted himself in his seat, "There is something else I can do. I just received a cheque for development aid from the federal government, something about repatriations for some harm done in a village back in the 1970s. In the same envelope is a proposal from America about accessing new mines in the North and palm oil fields in the South-West. We will need someone to supervise the whole process. Do you comprend?"

"We comprehend," Ernest said, in subtle correction. "So, you want to give these mines in exchange for aid money?"

Simon jabbed Ernest with his elbow. "Ernest please, it is not your whole mouth you must use to say everything."

"But who owns these mines?" Ernest persisted.

Eventually Ambrose said, "My friend, we are all corrupt, get your own."

"Is there anything else you can do for us? This contract seems high risk," Simon said, sensing his friend's hesitancy.

Ambrose looked at his bodyguard and said, "Tell Ṣadé to bring the contract files."

A short lady dressed all in peach came in. She was carrying grey folders stacked so high that it reached up to her neck. She struggled to walk as she carried them into the room.

"Yes, put them there," Ambrose said pointing to an empty chair next to him.

Ṣadé heaved the files on the chair, bending over to grab some that had spilled onto the floor. After she had finished cleaning up, she left the room quietly, leaving behind a long sillage of lavender. Simon watched her peach-clad bottom as she left the room.

"Ehn hen, now that the lovely Ṣadé has left, we men can talk business. Here are the undesirabilities. Some of these even pay in Naira. I know I had promised you dollars but that is the way of the cocoa. If you choose any of these, the margin is low but the advantage is that there is no oversight. The governor doesn't care about these *ikpakere* contracts," Ambrose chuckled deeply which made his belly vibrate joyfully along.

Simon had spotted some details of the contracts from when Ṣadé dropped some of the files. Sensing opportunity, he spoke first, "What about something to do with education? My friend here used to own a bookshop," he pointed to Ernest who was still too shocked by the pivot in the contract talk to react.

"Yes, we have some NYSC contracts. You can supply books and that kind of thing," Ambrose said.

Later on the way home, Simon explained to his friend, "These National Youth Service Corp contracts may not bring much money but they go on forever. Every graduate has to do national youth service so we will always be able to collect money from it, just wait my friend," Simon said excitedly as he swerved to avoid a street hawker.

———

One afternoon, Ernest ran into Démì giving Ìní advice on the living room floor. This was now a regular occurrence in their home. Ìní sitting on the floor, looking up at her brother while he doled out advice on anything from how to fold her clothes to how to call Daddy for help in public.

This day his advice was about how to run a home. "When you have your own place, you should not move," he said sagely.

Ìní nodded looking up at him.

"Because you need boxes to move and mouses live in boxes," Démì added.

"Mice," said Ernest sharply. "Plural of mouse is mice." He now knew they were talking about their frequent moves and he felt guilty.

"Children, I am building us a new house. It is two plots of land, very big. We will have our own space and there will be no need to move on Thursdays. I'll take you to look at the land after school tomorrow."

Ernest had bought two plots of land with his money from the NYSC contracts and he had started to plan their next move.

———

Grace entered the lift and pressed the ground floor button. It was 6 a.m. Too early for anybody to be up. In her haze of early morning confusion, she pressed the basement button. She tried again. The sharp stench of stale urine sneaked across her nostrils. Her nose twinged in response and her left eye watered. She tried not to breathe, feeling the smell go straight to her brain. She rarely took the lift for fear of the possibilities of faecal and urinal matter she might find there.

She exited the lift and made her way out of the estate, and turned right into Longfellow road, the main road leading out of their estate in Peckham.

She had been staying with BB for a month now. It was hell on wheels. There were currently eight people living in the two-bedroom flat. Having been accused of stealing BB's Müller rice pudding earlier that morning, which would no doubt be followed by another grudge, Grace had quickly made her way out of the flat. *Why was BB looking for a dessert at five in the morning anyway?* In any case, Grace was hoping to move out soon.

She walked past the teal-coloured estates on her right and the brown-coloured ones on her left. At the end of the road, she turned right instead of left to go the long way around. A couple of weeks back, she'd had an unpleasant altercation with the neighbourhood delinquents. They were mostly teenagers who talked tough and smoked on the low walls surrounding the estate.

A few of them had followed her asking her to help them buy cigarettes from the Asda, after she refused, they had all followed her, threatening her with sticks. She managed to escape them by running towards a well-lit area near the corner shop.

As she made her way to her early morning shift at the hospital, she thought about how she needed to make her way out of Babátúndé estate. *But how?*

She was now a full-fledged nurse on a rolling temporary contract. She couldn't afford it on her salary now and she didn't know if Gary would be able to renew her contract.

Grace stood outside the phone booth. She was waiting for the man inside to finish his phone call. She stood in a conspicuous place in his line of vision and shifted when he shifted. She had been waiting for twenty minutes; after ten she had started to stare him down. It was particularly artic tonight for October and the new coat she had just bought from the market looked like a duvet but protected like a sheet.

She tapped her foot impatiently. She looked at the man again. He pulled his flat cap down low and ignored her. She hadn't eaten dinner yet. She'd gone straight from work to the phone booth to try to call Ernest.

Maybe I will grab a KFC, she thought. Oh wait, that was the money for next week's stew. It was a hostile environment at home so she tried to be in the kitchen as little as possible. Every week, she cooked stew and used it as a staple for the week's meals. Unfortunately, the price for a KFC two-piece chicken meal or a burger was about the same as a whole pot of stew. *Why were these fast foods so expensive anyway?*

She caught a waft of the KFC again across the sidewalk from the phone booth, someone had just gone in and left the door ajar. The nearest other telephone box was down an alley she didn't like, plus it was the opposite way from the tube station, she'd have to double back to go home. The sharp tail of the chilly wind caught her exposed ankles and she pulled her coat tighter. She was desperate to call Ernest and ask his advice about the problems she was having at BB's.

If she went home, there was another phone booth nearer the house but it was too close to the rougher part of the estate, and where they had murdered that Jamaican boy.

She shivered again and started to walk away. The man clanged his way out of the box. On hearing the noise, Grace looked back. As she walked past him towards the phone booth, he sniffed and she thought she caught the reflective glint of tears running down his cheeks.

———

Gary called Grace into his office. "How long have you been in the UK now?"

"Two years," Grace said, wondering what this was about.

Gary was a dedicated, passionate man with silvery white hair, in his mid-fifties. He was always nice to Grace and always made a point of asking about her family. He was divorced but obsessed with his two daughters whom he saw very little of, so he often empathised with Grace about missing her family. Most of these conversations were one-sided though, with Grace offering very little explanation to Gary's sympathetic enquiries.

"I know you have finished your adaptation course and in theory we can hire you as a nurse now but I'm afraid there is no budget to extend your contract anymore. The good news is you've been here long enough now that can find work elsewhere as a full nurse. They just have to get you a visa. Do you follow?"

Grace was shocked into silence. She was afraid this day might come.

Scratching his wide chin, Gary said, "I'm really sorry, Grace. I know it's not what you want to hear. If there is anything I can do for you…"

Grace was still silent so he continued, "Have you looked in the *Nursing Times*? Do you know where to look for work? Sometimes, the *Royal College of Nursing* paper also advertises, we have a subscription so we always have those in the foyer. You can ask Sandra." He coughed and took a long sip of his tea.

Grace, thinking he had finished talking, turned to walk away, but Gary added, "Some of the big hospitals as well will advertise in newspapers so you can find adverts there too, there's always some free ones on the train."

"Thank you, Gary," Grace said kindly and walked out the door.

———

Grace turned the map upside down. She wanted to sit down, her left toes were crying. She could feel the coolness of the red perforated metallic seat at the station through her thin blue suit. Human resources had sent a lot of information. The pictorial map was not helping and neither were the written directions: 'Turn west as you exit the station'. *What does that mean*?

She looked at her watch, she still had plenty of time. Grace turned the map the right way up again. She finally took off her problematic left shoe. The smallest toe had been trying to escape, having been wedged in for far too long.

She looked up and saw the sign for the hospital near the side exit of the station. Her left toes having forgiven her, she put her shoe back on and soldiered ahead.

The instructions said she could also take the bus, but she didn't want to pay for anything additional, besides it was only supposed to be a twenty-minute walk and she had come in plenty of time.

She noticed the people here also walked fast like in London, so she quickened her pace. She turned left and saw a huge grey castle. As she followed the road wrapped around the castle at the start of the high street, she marvelled at the castle's monotone. In my country, it would be multicoloured, to emphasise its opulence, she thought.

The road got steeper as she rounded the front of the castle, so she slowed down. She looked at her watch, it had been five minutes. She looked at the map again, she was starting to see the shops marked on the map, she couldn't find all of them but she found some.

After fifteen more minutes of twisting and turning the map to find her way, she finally made it to the hospital. It was magnificent, very clean and well presented. She went to the toilet first to dry out her patches of sweat and placed some tissue underneath both armpits and waited for the perspiration to soak through. After a few minutes, she took them out and went to reception to announce herself and wait for Jemima Clarke.

———

Grace tried not to skip. She wasn't a skipper. That was not an interview, it was more like a chat. Jemima or Jemi, as she preferred to be called, was so lovely. Grace had joked about it being similar to the Nigerian name, Yẹmí, but she didn't think Jemi got her joke.

Grace got the impression that Jemi was no nonsense despite her outward loveliness.

So, when can you start?" Jemi said as she brought their conversation to a close.

"Immediately, Ma," Grace said using the Nigerian affectation reserved for older people as a sign of respect. Correcting herself she said, "I mean thank you, I can start immediately."

"As part of your package, you will be housed in the nurses' hostel next to the hospital. You will receive training and your visa will be extended as long as you have a contract."

"Thank you so much."

"We will send your welcome pack in the post. HR will contact you about the arrangements for the nurses' hostel. Like I said, I don't know how much it is but it will come out of your salary."

They had both got on famously with similar work ethics and total devotion to their families.

Grace did start to skip now as she headed back to the station, she had a feeling she would like Windsor.

———

Grace hung around by the only phone in the nurses' hostel, waiting for the dark-haired beauty to finish her call, she was speaking a language Grace did not understand. She turned around briefly to acknowledge that she knew Grace was waiting, moving the handset to her right hand and signalling with her left to say five minutes. She went back to her phone call, speaking in a soft undulating language, her halo of brown afro hair shaking as she spoke.

"Jambo," the dark-haired beauty greeted Grace hello and walked past.

"Hello," Grace responded back quietly, recognising the only word of Swahili she knew.

"Are you from Ghana?" the dark-haired beauty enquired. "I'm Florence…" she stretched out her hand to meet Grace's.

"I'm Grace. No, I'm Nigerian. Were you speaking Swahili?"

"It's Kiswahili. I'm from Kenya. I was just calling my husband and children. Are you new in the hostel?"

"Yes, I start work tomorrow as a cardiac nurse."

"Congratulations! I work as a surgical nurse. I've been here one year so if you need anything…" she waved her hands expansively. "You can use those phones over there to call out if you have a phone card or you can get people to call you if you write down the number. Do you have children?"

"Yes, I have two. They live in Nigeria with my husband."

"Oh, how lovely. My three children are with my mother in our village near Mombasa but my husband works in Nairobi. Around this time of the evening, after dinner, the phones are usually busy and at weekends but if your husband can be up early before seven, then that is the best time to call home or if you can work through your lunch and take a break later, it is quiet here then."

"That is good advice, thank you. Sorry I've forgotten your name?"

"It's Florence, and yours?"

"Grace."

"Ok, Grace. Good night. See you in the hospital. You can find me in Building C, if you need anything."

Florence's brown halo looked like a hat from behind as she walked away down the corridor.

———

The day the Àlejòs moved out of the church into their newly built house was torrential. The builders had finished on a Thursday but Ernest waited until Saturday when the children were not in school to move them in, a decision he later regretted.

Halfway through building, he had started to run out of money so he focused on finishing and roofing three of the rooms and the bathroom. *The rest I will build slowly as I get more money from the NYSC contracts*, he reasoned.

The Saturday morning started out with a short downpour. After about an hour, figuring it was over, Ernest started loading the car. He had bought a Jeep with his NYSC contract money.

They unloaded the first car load of stuff into one of the rooms and went back for the rest. The children seemed to be enjoying riding in the rain with their father. By the time, they came back to unload the second time, the rain had flooded through from the unroofed parts of the house and drenched their belongings. Ernest felt like he had failed. He realised the architect had made a serious error in judgement and had failed to wall off one of the rooms, causing water to flow through to the rest.

Realising they couldn't stay there, Ernest and the kids loaded the car with what they could and drove back to the church.

My love,

I am very sorry to have to tell you this by letter but Baba went to be with the Lord last Sunday.

I have tried calling you but some white woman kept picking up, I think the call was getting crossed with another line.

I have spoken to Mama and she is doing ok, as are your brothers.

I know you do not have your right-to-remain papers yet or the money to come home. I want to reassure you that I will be at the funeral with my sisters and their husbands so you will be well represented. I wish I could comfort you in person.

Ps. Have you found somewhere to do your hair that is nearer to Windsor? Hope you don't have to travel the two hours to Peckham again.

The children send their greetings. Demi is doing well in boarding school. His friend, Ortega, is also a boarder there.

We have fixed the leak in the new house and the architect has completed enough rooms such that it is now liveable. We moved in at the end of last month.

Still in love with you,

Ernest

The only time Grace mentioned the death of her father to anyone was to Florence and it was entirely by accident.

Florence had found her in the canteen lost in thought and staring at some packs of pretzels.

"Oh, you like those? I always find they make my throat dry. We don't have these back home."

Grace, not hearing her, was silent. Florence manoeuvred herself sideways to interrupt Grace's line of vision and repeated, "I said, we don't have these back home." There was something poignant in the way Florence said 'home' that resonated with Grace. This time, she did hear and involuntary tears threatened her lids. She reached inside her pockets for the tissues she always carried. She hurried to catch the tears before they fell. It was too late. Florence had seen them. With quiet sympathy, she hugged Grace.

Silently, they walked through the cafeteria until they were in the nurses' changing rooms. Grace, who hated explaining herself, knew this time she had to, so she said simply, "My father died."

Without further words, Florence hugged her and let her cry. After a while, Grace said, "I can't go home, not yet. I can't think. The only times my head feels clear is when I am thinking about my father. Everything else floors me and makes me feel overwhelmed, and I can't go home," she dissolved further into tears and placed her head on Florence's shoulder and sobbed silently.

"I am sorry," said Florence. She was happy to be the recipient of her friend's unburdening. She also wondered why Grace could not go home. There was an unspoken code amongst immigrants where their immigration status is never discussed and in the quiet unravelling of her friend, Florence honoured that code. Rather, she held Grace in the stillness of that moment and let her cry.

Grace, who seemed so strong like she could handle anything, who looked at you through her almond-shaped eyes, absorbing and listening, like a spongy wall. "It gets easier, I lost my father at a young age. I was eight years old and it was my uncle that told me. From what you told me about your father, you are giving your children the education he never gave you. So, in a way, it is a good thing you are not home because that's what you're busy doing." Realising she may not be saying the right things, Florence went quiet for a while, then finally said, "I'm sorry about the death of your father. To lose a parent is never easy."

"I just have this pain in my chest when I think about him. It's just, when someone dies, where does our love go?"

Chapter 6

"Ọkọ mi. You're so late, my flight landed five hours ago."

"I'm so sorry. That Lagos–Ibadan expressway, there was a spillage on the way, a truck spilled metal rods onto the tarmac." Ernest started to carry Grace's bags and walk ahead urgently.

Grace watched him in the baking heat of July and suddenly felt bad. She had gotten used to the more predictable life abroad, she realised she had unfairly blamed him for the lateness.

When they reached the car, she waited for him to load the bags, then embraced him warmly. Touched, Ernest wept quietly.

"I've missed you!" Grace's words were muffled into his left shoulder. "How are my children?"

"They are very good. They are with your brother. We will pick them up on the way home."

It was night time before they finally reached their house. A gossipy cousin had spread the news about Grace's return, such that, the entire extended family was waiting at her brother's when she got there to pick up the children. As they entered the compound, a distinct smell of puff-puff, that doughy saccharine smell that accompanied most Nigerian parties, wafted out to greet them. Then out came Démì, wielding a plastic spoon stained with jollof rice, followed closely by Ìní, overcome with the emotion of seeing her mother.

The whole family embraced, Ernest tearing up repeatedly and Grace managing to stay stoic through all of it, absorbing and trying to remember it all frame-by-frame.

Démì had a lot of questions and wanted to know everything about her journey in the airplane, calling it 'through the clouds' until one of the adults told him to shut up. He had a latent fascination with cloud formation and talked endlessly about wanting to be a climatologist, having lately been learning about different professions at his boarding school. Ernest didn't have the heart to tell him the weather didn't vary a great deal enough in Nigeria to base an entire career on it. Besides, he changed his mind often, sometimes he talked about wanting to be an engineer, other times a teacher.

On the ride home, it was quiet and when they got to their house, everyone was tired. They sat in the living room for a little bit, Grace wanting to spend more time with the four of them, but Ìní and Démì sat there and stared at their mother, four years of distance having decreased their rapport. It broke Grace's heart, she realised she didn't really know them.

After a short while of awkward silence, Ernest ushered them to bed.

Unsettled, Grace complained to Ernest that perhaps if she had called enough, her children would know her and be familiar with how to relate to her, instead of this yawning divide threatening to swallow them whole.

"They're just tired," Ernest reassured her but inside he realised that perhaps she was right, in the intervening four years, the kids simply had gotten used to not having her around.

———

"Sometimes you're talking and you think you're speaking English but they don't understand you."

"Why don't they understand you, Mummy?" said Ìní.

"Because even though we're all speaking English, we have something called accents or we use different words. Like your Daddy and I are from different parts of Yorùbá land so when I say 'ótì', your Dad says 'rárá', but they both mean 'no'.

"Oooooh," said Démì recognising what she meant. Switching tacks, he said, "Do you have a car, Mummy?"

"Yes, like Daddy's jeep," added Ìní.

"No. I don't have a car but I take the train, and when I go to London to do my hair, sometimes I take something called 'the tube'. It is underground, you go into a hole in the ground and you come out of another hole so it's hard to know directions when you're always underground."

"Like a soldier ant," Démì said solemnly, now worrying that his mummy may get lost in the underground maze. He imagined lots of sand everywhere like when him and Ìní would study ants carrying sugar, worming their way in and out of holes in their backyard.

———

“I think we should think about moving the family to England,” said Grace one evening while her and Ernest were lying in bed.

There was silence. It dragged on and in the thick of it, Ernest tilted his shoulder slightly. Finally, he calmly said, “You were only supposed to go for a few years to better ourselves.”

“I know but what am I coming back to here? The ministry has retired me in absentia. I’ve now built up another career and pension in the UK. If I come back here, I’ll be starting again.”

“But you want me to start again? I’m forty-seven, Grace!” Realising he was raising his voice, he breathed and tried again. “You told me yourself people who are doctors here are starting again over there as early morning cleaners and bus drivers. I’m not willing to do that, Gracious.” Thinking of how much he’d been through selling the bookstore and still waiting for the money, then starting again with the NYSC contract work, he shook his head. “I’m just not willing,” he added.

“But would you do it for your children?” Grace said.

She had him there. His face dropped and this time the silence gripped the room, Grace could feel the temperature drop in response. Attempting to raise the temperature to a more ambient feel, Grace added gently, “Ọkọ mi, look at these children, if they continue like this, their education will stall. Démì will go for his JSS exams next year and then he’ll be looking at university in three short years. University teachers are always on strike here, students are out of school more than they are in school, teenagers wandering the street for months with nothing to do. Is this what he's heading towards? I don't want that to happen to our Démì."

She dropped the silence again. It felt icy. This time, she let it stretch out. Ernest, now fully thawed in his thinking, kissed her on the forehead and turned over to sleep.

Grace stayed awake a little bit longer, turning the future over in her mind.

———

The next day in the car, Ernest started the topic of moving again without preamble.

"But what would I do there? The contracting business is just starting to work." An okada zoomed past carrying a woman with two chickens on her lap.

"What is the alternative Ernest, ehn? This split family where my children don't know me?"

"My life is here. Once you have your papers, you can visit more often or the children can visit you," Ernest said reasonably.

"That's not enough! I only have four weeks of annual leave. I cannot see my children one month a year."

Ernest knew he was losing this battle but the thought of starting again in another country terrified him. He wanted his wife back but he knew what that would cost him and the cost to the future of their children if their family remained split.

Plus, it was Grace's second week and he was starting to get annoyed with her complaints. She complained when things weren't working as they should, the electrician who came to fix some appliances and was three hours late, the power cut that lasted four days at the beginning of her first week and their five-hour wait at the mechanic with promises that didn't pan out. Eventually, he had to tell her quite harshly that she needed to remember the pace of life here was quite different and not to expect the same dovetail structure of her life in the nurses' hostel.

Grace, on the other hand, was aware she had limited time to spend with her children. Everything seemed to be racing by her so she found herself to be very impatient with everything. She also struggled with getting used to her husband's subversive reactions. He didn't like it when she suggested possible better ways of doing things or if she tried to pay for things. It had never been a big deal before she left for England, they were used to shuffling change between them, having next to nothing.

Now he even complained about her vernacular, how much she had changed, she wasn't exactly sure what changes he was talking about. He accused her of acting against their culture. She also found herself rather pole-axed about this attitude of not wanting to move. It had been their long-term plan for their family but now he claimed she could work for a few more years and then move back. On top of that, all he wanted to talk about were his NYSC contracts.

On the plane back, Grace held her head in her hands and contemplated what the future might look like.

It had been an expensive trip. If Ernest didn't move, she didn't think she'd be able to afford to come back for another two years at least. That was too long to even contemplate being away from her children.

At least they'd have the pictures. She smiled as she thought about the pictures she had left hanging on the wall in their rooms.

———

"Florence my sister, how are you?" said Grace.

"Very good, I haven't seen you for a long time," said Florence.

"I have been preparing o, my family is coming," Grace smiled through her words.

"Ehhhhh, congratulations my sister." Florence leaned forward to hug her friend across the lunch table. "When are they coming? Is that why I have not seen you? You have moved out of the nurses' hostel." The last sentence was more of a conclusion than a question.

"They're coming next year. I'm so happy my family will be in one place... I don't sleep anymore. All I do is think about my little Ìní. She is ten now. I've missed most of her life. She was five when I left. When I went home last year, it was like she didn't recognise me."

"I'm sorry, my sister. My children are the same. They look at me with... suspicion. But my husband thinks I'm talking crazy," said Florence. She bit into an apple and chewed looking at her friend.

Grace played with her rice and stew with the end of her fork. She had lost concentration again, daydreaming of when her family will be united. She was most worried for Ìní, who seemed to be rather sensitive and perhaps would not be able to adjust to yet another move.

"So where are you living now?" Florence said, finishing her apple.

"I'm living in one of the flats owned by the hospital – Southwell Courts. Jemima helped me to apply."

"I didn't even know they had one of those. Maybe I can apply when my family moves over."

Grace came out of her daydream and had continued eating again. "Yes, let me know. You'll need it to apply for visas for them. You'll need to show that you have a place for them to stay when they come here."

Finishing her lunch. Grace got up and announced she was going back to work. Florence watched her friend as she walked away, the dark cloud hanging around her friend since they met had finally lifted.

Part 2, 1998

Chapter 7
Windsor, Berkshire, UK

The Àlejòs moved in winter, it was convenient and near the start of the school year.

Grace had a frantic morning having just come off the night shift, before she took the train to Gatwick airport. At the front of the crowds, she stood clutching the sweaters she had bought them, having not been able to afford proper winter coats. She played with the frayed edges of the grey one she had bought for Ernest, she hoped he would not mind, that was all she could afford at the charity shop. The softness of the jumper soothed her as she played with it.

Her mind went to their last argument before she left Àkúrẹ́. She was nervous about him adjusting here, given he had expressly said he did not want to move. She hoped it would be worth it or that he would look at their children and see why they were doing this.

The first person she saw was Ìní. Her skinny frame came rushing out ahead of the throng of people in arrivals. She noticed Ìní's hair, Ernest had done it in single-braid extensions. *Good, it will last weeks*, she thought. They wouldn't need to hazard the long visit to Peckham, which meant a day off, which also meant Grace wouldn't be earning money while she was there.

Sometimes, she felt odd thinking about time in terms of money.

Grace hugged them all with Ìní clutching onto all their legs, she squeezed Ernest to keep him from going into full-blown tears, his eyes having been glistening earlier as he blinked rapidly to hide them.

On the train home, Ernest updated her on their fateful trip to Lagos. The bus from Àkúrẹ́ had broken down somewhere after Ìkirè thus dumping everybody in the small town famous for its mashed plantain delicacy. They'd had to improvise to find a way to get to Lagos for their flight later that night. Luckily, the nearest city was Ìbàdàn and it was easy to charter a car from there. Grace listened and smiled, concluding they made it here, despite Ernest's dramatic arcs in the story.

Somewhere around Harlington, just outside Berkshire, it started to snow.

———

As they stepped off the platform at Windsor, Ìní got her first smell of winter. It was a wet, slightly astringent smell. It reminded her of clothes freshly washed with *Omo*.

When they got home and had lunch, Ìní and Démì got restless and wanted to go out in the snow. Ernest and Grace had their heads together in a conversation that felt like it would go on forever.

"Mummy, can we go out and see the snow?" Ìní said.

"No, it is too cold," Grace said.

"But Mummy we have never seen snow before," Démì pleaded.

"We want to touch it, it's beautiful!" Ìní added.

"Let them go and see the snow *now*," Ernest pleaded.

"Oya, go," Grace relented.

A few minutes later, they returned. "Why have you come back?" Grace said.

"It's cold," Démì said.

"Well, that's the downside of beautiful things, sometimes they are cold," said Grace.

———

The flat in Southwell Court thrummed with renewed filial energy. Grace felt a new sense of completeness.

In the cosy heat of the flat, their sweaters now ditched on the arm of the sofa, Ernest moved closer and put his arm around Grace occasionally leaning in to kiss her. She leaned her head on his shoulder and they passively watched TV.

"So maybe I can go look for work tomorrow?" Ernest said.

"Ehn, rárá o. You can wait until after the weekend. You just came *now*. Let us enjoy the weekend."

Later that night, leaning back against the headboard in their room, she watched Ernest sitting on the edge of the bed in only his pyjama bottoms, scouting the newspaper for jobs. She missed this old evening routine of theirs.

"What is GSOH?" Ernest said.

"Oh, those are not job adverts. I think that is the personal section."

"But it says, '*Man wanted'*."

"Is the print very small?"

"Yes, it is smaller than the others."

"That section is not for you. We will go out tomorrow and look on the high street."

———

The next morning, Grace and Ernest traipsed the streets asking for application forms. At the end of Peascod street, they stopped and sat on one of the benches that wrapped around the castle walls. Grace sat next to him, opposite them was a McDonald's and a small Chinese restaurant.

"Shall we try in there as well?" Grace said with some slight hesitation.

"What is McDonald?"

"It's like Mr Biggs."

"Oh, must be expensive then."

"It is o, we cannot afford it."

Ernest spent the next couple of days filling in application forms and then on Wednesday when Grace was at work, he started returning them.

———

"Hello, is that Mr Aleyjo?"

"Daaaaaaaaaddy!" Démì yelled. "Telephone!"

"Who is it? I have told you to always ask."

"Hello? Yes, this is Mr Àlejò."

"I'm calling from McDonald's. Can you come in for an interview on Thursday?"

"Yes, I can."

"Two o'clock ok?"

"Yes, thank you."

———

"That Mr Biggs place called today." Ernest said to Grace later that night.

"What Mr Biggs place?"

"McDonald."

"Oh, what did they say?"

"They want me to come in for an interview on Thursday."

"That's good. Did any of the others call?" Grace said, now putting on her scarf for the night and going through her night-time routine.

"No, I haven't heard from them yet."

"It's been two weeks. Maybe we should start applying for some other ones."

"Ok, I'll go out again tomorrow to collect more application forms."

"Maybe we can try Slough."

———

McDonald's could only give Ernest a part-time job so he got another at a meat locker.

"Good morning, my name is Ernest. The agency sent me."

"Welcome Ernest. I'm Asim. I will introduce you to John. He's the team leader."

Asim put down his headset and led Ernest down the stairs and into a long hallway with big grey lockers on either side. About halfway down, he turned left into one of the lockers, Ernest felt the change in temperature and audibly shuddered.

"Ooh, did you not bring a coat?" Asim said.

Ernest pulled his clothes tighter and hugged himself. The thin blue jacket was all he had. Grace had bought it at a charity shop. It looked warm but most of the stuffing had fallen out, such that Ernest still found bits of it amongst his clothes every day.

In the icy locker, several headless carcasses hung upside down from metal hooks, with streams of crimson fluid running into the drains below. Careful not to slip, Ernest walked gingerly as he followed Asim deeper into the locker.

"Oh, here comes John," Asim said.

A broad-shouldered man with a gentle expression wearing a black puffa jacket was walking towards them and greeted Ernest with a handshake and a warm smile.

"Hi Ernest. I'm John."

"Hello, John."

"So, uh… Asim says the agency has sent you here for three days. We actually need someone for longer so we'll see how you do."

"Ok," Ernest said.

"Some guys quit last Friday so we're uh… in a bit of a bind. These are the daily orders and quotas we have to fill," John pointed to several sheets stapled to a cork message board behind him. "So, your job is to pack the meat the guys are uh… cutting, move them into boxes and then uh… make sure the labels are right."

"Ok," Ernest said.

"You get paid per box packed. Any mistakes you won't get paid. Any questions?"

"No."

"You will be working with uh… Joe and uh… Peter. Just follow them and you'll be fine. Asim will sign your timesheet every evening before you leave."

———

Démì was astonished how kids spoke to teachers in school. It was a far cry from the reign of terror teachers imposed in his secondary school back home.

He watched one boy say, 'That's nonsense' to a teacher and not get spanked. Back in his school in Àkúrẹ́, that would have been twenty lashes or pick-pin punishment until one of his legs gave out.

That evening when he got home, he shared with his mum what he had witnessed in school that day.

Grace's response was to shrug. "Yes, they don't punish children here."

She seemed preoccupied so Démì left her alone and went to his room.

Ìní had also noticed a trend of her parents feeling preoccupied lately. They were always whispering in corners and having long talks. She took to slinkering around the house and hiding in her room a lot, like Démì.

———

Ìní stopped to pull her socks up, tears dropping on her knuckles. She tried to keep on the narrow pavement as Grace had warned. Her fingers were cold and for a minute, she was distracted by the moving clouds emanating from her nose, then she remembered the words of the bullies. Her chest contracted at the memory of their harsh words as they followed her from third period into the toilet. She had no idea how many of them followed her, she just kept walking, their voices getting louder when they got closer, then lower when they retreated. As she reached the toilet, she dashed inside a stall.

From behind the safety of the stall, she had counted at least six pairs of shoes, the others were hidden from view, but she could hear their taunts from the other side.

"*What is wrong with your hair?*"

"*What are you doing in there?*"

"*Why is your uniform weird?*"

"*Did you not tell your parents to buy it from the store?*"

"*Did you bring it from Africa?*"

Laughter followed by questions, then more laughter.

"*Why are you wearing socks?*"

"*Do they not have tights in Africa?*"

"*Why do you speak English*?"

"*What kind of name is Ìní?*"

"*Did they mean to name you ini't?*"

"*You smell!*"

After the bell rang, they disappeared for fourth period but she stayed in the stall, paralysed with fear in case one of them lingered behind. After fourth period, some came back with more questions and yet more jeering laughter. She climbed on top of the seat, hoping they would go away. It worked. She started on her homework to pass the time.

After the final period, she slinked out into the open winter air.

———

"Daddy, some children in school were asking me why my family moved here."

It was Saturday and in a rare twist of things, the whole family was home.

"What did you tell them?"

"I told them we came to join my mummy."

"But do you know why we came to Britain?"

"No," Ìní scratched her nose, sensing a lecture coming on.

Ernest put down his copy of the *Windsor Observer*.

"Well, Britain colonised Nigeria and we got independence in 1960, and after we joined the Commonwealth. It also meant that we could come here and they could go to our country freely so that happened for years. I told you about our friends, the Tìmáyọ̀s?"

"The veterinarian?"

"Yes, him and his wife studied here during that time when there was free movement between the countries. But when Nigeria got independence and the corrupt came into power, and the wasting of resources meant that there was very little for the little people, when people started to escape the poverty, it was easier to come to a place where they already had a connection and had shared the so-called wealth for so long. You see?"

"Yes, I see," said Ìní.

"So, when your classmate asks you, that is what you should tell them.

"Ok, Daddy."

The blond boy with the fuzzy moustache turned around to face Démì. He looked him up and down then said, "So you're from Nigeria? What's that like?"

Shocked that the blond boy was talking so openly during English literature class instead of passing a note like Démì and his friend Ortega used to do, Démì looked behind, thinking he must be talking to someone else. Eventually, when no one else looked up let alone answered, Démì said, "It's like here, roads, schools, offices and buildings."

"You know what I imagine Africa is like, lots of dust and villages and thatched buildings," fuzzy moustache said.

"No, I will bring you pictures and you can see where I used to live and what our city is like," Démì said.

"You lived in a city? Cool, I'd love to see the pictures." After a short pause, he whispered, "Why don't you wear your blazer? Are you trying to be naughty like us? That's why we don't wear ties, to wind up Mr Daltonflower," fuzzy moustache continued.

The bell rang and he followed Démì out of the class. Realising, he was still waiting for an answer, Démì said, "My parents don't have the means. After they paid for me and my sister's uniform, we didn't have enough left to buy a blazer so I have to wait until they have money. Plus, we didn't have blazers in my boarding school back in Nigeria."

Embarrassed by Démì's transparent answer, fuzzy moustache boy crept away to join his friends.

Another boy who had been listening to their exchange, Riko, moved closer to Démì and said, "When I first moved here, my mum also could not afford the blazer so I had to do two terms without it."

"Hello, I'm Démì," Démì introduced himself the way Grace had instructed, looking Riko in the eye and smiling.

Riko was impressed by Démì's quietly confident manner and continued talking to him about the differences between boarding schools here in the UK and where Démì was from. Did Démì know it was for rich people, which is why you confused Martin and he walked off.

———

"Do you feel like you know Mum?" Ìní asked Démì one day.

"Yeah, somewhat. I do. Why do you ask?" Démì was reading a comic book that Riko had given him and he didn't want to be bothered.

"Well, I don't really understand her."

Alerted to the fact that his little sister may be having some trouble, she now had his full attention. "What don't you understand? Is something wrong?" said Démì kindly.

"Well, I don't really know her. Remember she left when I was five," looking down and shrugging, Ìní added, "I don't remember her much."

Realising he'd taken for granted he'd had seven years with their mother, Démì sat up straight on his bed. "Well, what do you want to know?"

"Yesterday she yelled at me and I'm not even sure why."

"What were you doing?"

"I wasn't doing anything. She said I left my books on the table and I needed to tidy up. I only had one book there, the rest were Dad's."

"Oh, well you know that's because she gets tired. She works twelve-hour shifts and I've noticed when she's tired, you just need to stay out of her way, ok?"

"Ok. The punishment didn't match the crime, you know?"

Démì started laughing. "I know where you heard that, it was on *The Bill*," referring to the TV show they had both been watching of late.

———

Grace and Ernest were huddled in the kitchen again talking finances and house stuff. Démì and Ìní stayed out of their way.

"They extended my contract to three weeks," Ernest said.

"What do you think my love?" Grace said, knowing he hated his job at the meat locker. He was not used to the cold.

"It is good for us because we need the money but I cannot lie to you my darling, it is bitterly cold."

"Do you think you can do it for three more weeks?"

"Yes kẹ̀, this is for our family," Ernest said.

"Thank you," Grace said and kissed him.

"I just wanted to check you are ok to work this weekend. You are always the only one volunteering." Lugo the head nurse said, looking at Grace and searching her face for clues that she didn't mind working so much. They were sitting in the nurses' break room.

Earlier that morning, a most awkward staff meeting had ended in Lugo having to pick two people randomly when no one would volunteer for the Easter bank holiday shift.

"Yes, it is ok." Grace said.

"Are you sure?"

"Yes, Lugo I am sure."

"Ok, thank you. It is double pay. We will pay you double. These agency staff you know? They are spoilt and there is a dispute with the agency so we have to sort that out. Don't even get me started on these locum doctors – always complaining, never satisfied."

"Ok, I told Mrs Hilling I would come back to check on her."

"Yes, of course. Sorry, patients first." Grace got up and walked towards the door. "Thank you!" Lugo yelled after her as the door swung shut behind her.

Then deciding he should check on his patients as well, Lugo followed her down the hall running to keep up. Grace sensing his approach, quickened her pace. At last, Lugo caught up and continued complaining about the locum doctors.

———

Grace had a notepad where she calculated their weekly expenses – blue for positive and red for negative. She hid it from Ernest because the balance was always negative and she did not want him to see it and feel guilty.

One day in haste leaving for an afternoon shift, she left it on the drawer. Ernest, a normally trusting sort, would never normally look through his wife's things but an open notebook covered in red scrawls certainly drew his attention.

He did not mention the incident to Grace, figuring she would tell him in her own time.

———

"I hate this tile," Ernest scrubbed vigorously at the errant tile. Ìní stood behind him watching. It was

Saturday morning. She had wandered into the kitchen to see what was for breakfast.

After standing there for a few minutes, then realising Ernest was holding a small trowel instead of a sponge as she had first thought, she backed off quietly into the adjoining living room. She was used to him cleaning when he was upset but a trowel signalled bigger problems.

How long do we have to wait for breakfast? Ìní thought grudgingly. There was no sign of Mum so guessing her mother had gone for an early shift, Ìní settled into the sunken end of their grey sofa and started watching SMTV live, to wait out Ernest and his frustrations with the tile.

———

"These supermarket trips to Slough are getting too expensive," Grace said to Ernest one afternoon.

"Ehn why don't we shop here in Windsor? I have been meaning to ask you about that. The trolley is very heavy when we have to move all that food back. Is there not a supermarket here?" said Ernest.

"There is but we cannot afford to shop there. Slough is the closest option."

"So, if Slough is getting too expensive, what are our options?"

"Florence said we can try Peckham. Things are much cheaper there. Aunty BB used to buy a whole box of chicken and other foodstuffs and store it in the deep freezer. That way we don't need to go that often. But ọkọ mi, before we do this, we have to find the money for a deep freezer first."

"Ah, how much will that cost us? Can we get it on hire purchase?"

"They call it buy-now-pay-later. If we get it now, we will save a lot on buying food and by this time next year, we will have finished paying it off."

"Ok, let us go tomorrow after work," Ernest said.

"What are you doing this weekend?"

Friday had rolled round again and here came the dreaded question – *what are you doing this weekend?* Ìní hated that question because she never knew what to say. Her weekends constituted of homework and watching TV with her parents but that was always met with blank stares or frowns from her classmates. So she had taken to leaving the conversation when the rounds of the offending questions started. The idea that you had to be doing something with your weekend was completely foreign to her. *What is wrong with being at home with your parents anyway*?

"We are getting a deep freezer," Ìní said, finally happy she had something to announce she was doing that weekend.

"What is a deep freezer?"

"It is a big freezer where we store extra food like stew and frozen meat." They had had one back in Àkúrẹ́ and Ìní and Démì had definitely noticed that Mummy did not have one in the flat when they arrived. They had just added it to the list of strange things in England along with other things like no ceiling fans, calling adults by their first names and talking back to the teacher.

———

That Saturday, when Grace and Ernest had gone to Peckham to buy food to fill their brand-new deep freezer, Démì and Ìní took a walk to the high street to explore their neighbourhood. They walked all the way up the hill, stopped at the green grocers, they stopped at the Theatre Royal and watched the rows of people going in for the matinee, and at the end of Peascod street, they saw the castle and marvelled at the size. They walked all the way up to the main entrance then turned back. Eventually they walked up to Eton bridge and stood watching River Thames below.

Someone tapped Ìní on the shoulder, interrupting her reminisce with Démì about his life back in boarding school. It was a boy and two girls from her geography class. She didn't really know them well except that they always sat near the door, were the last to come in and the first to leave. She switched to English and introduced Démì. After they left, Démì turned to her and said almost angrily, "Why did you tell them we were speaking Nigerian? That's not our language."

"Because I don't feel like explaining and I don't think they care anyway," Ìní said, moody at Démì's confrontation.

"We were speaking Yorùbá. If people ask you, that's what you should tell them."

"I don't think it matters," Ìní shrugged. "It is easier this way. People in school already think I'm weird. I don't feel like explaining whatever people find weird about me that day, it's tiring, it's like... like…" Ìní now frustrated, struggled to find her words.

"…like explaining your existence," Démì added, finally acquiescing. He didn't want to argue about it anymore.

———

Démì was now fourteen and liked to spend lots of time alone, brooding. He had taken after Ernest's tall frame and had joined the school rugby team, which had given him a wide athletic frame that made him larger than most boys his age.

He was acutely aware of people's reaction to him when he walked into places, such that he started to fold himself in such a way as to disarm people.

He was about to disappear into his room again, when Ernest called him.

"Démì, come here."

"Yes, sir."

"The school called and said you shouted at another boy in school today?" Démì kept his head bowed.

"Ehn? No answer – what's wrong with your mouth?"

"He kept calling me Démì."

"But that is your name. Is Démì not your name? Graaaaaaace! Come and listen to your son o."

Grace came in, shoes in hand. The first thing she did as she entered the flat from her shift was to take her shoes off. This was often followed by some rigorous hand washing.

"What happened?" Grace walked past them into the adjoining kitchen to complete her daily ritual.

"He shouted at another boy in school today and the other boy tried to beat him, they had to separate them," said Ernest, now raising his voice above the gushing noise of the tap.

"What?! I have told you, you cannot do that at these white schools. They will expel you. Do you hear? They will give you an expulsion!" said Grace. Démì was looking down in catatonic silence. Calling him by his full name, "Adémọlá! What is the matter?"

Démì kept his head down. He didn't want to go into why he now preferred to be called by his full name at school. He felt like he was losing himself in this new culture. Being called Démì now seemed to him a casual throwaway diminutive used by perfect strangers who didn't share his culture. Yet, he didn't mind that his family called him Démì, he reasoned they could do that, because they knew the literal meaning of Adémọlá and could afford the luxury of shortening it.

Catching his thoughts wandering, he rearranged his stance and demeanour into contriteness and continued to listen to his parents' reprimand.

———

Démì was starting to get wary of asking his parents for money for every little need: school trips, deodorant, shaving stuff and other such minor things. Especially because he knew they didn't have extra money and he saw the look on his mother's face everytime he asked. He could see the machinations behind her eyes calculating what they would have to let go of in order to give him what he asked. His father managed to remain zen through these moments except for the occasional leg shake that betrayed his agitation.

They always came up with the money, usually after a few days, but a few weeks later, Démì would also find out, by his own clever deductions, what the family had given up in return and it always made him feel guilty.

He knew from Riko that a man in Martin's neighbourhood had been giving students from their school odd jobs in exchange for money. They were not yet sixteen so it was not quite legal.

Démì tried plotting how he could get away from home one afternoon to go and get himself a job. So he told his parents about an after-school revision club and that afternoon, he followed Martin to Mr Genova's café to get himself a job washing plates for £1.50 an hour.

Martin went in to collect the money for his cigarettes – his pocket money from his parents was never quite enough to keep up his smoking habit so he supplemented it with cleaning tables at Mr Genova's so he could buy cigarettes at the gas station opposite their school.

"Hello Mr Genova, this is my friend, Démì. He is also sixteen. He'd like to wash plates too for some extra bit of money."

"Good afternoon, Démì. Call me Bruno," Mr Genova was a wide man with a generous smile. He wore a blue polo shirt that was taut over his broad shoulders. His wide-set eyes brimming with glee at yet more cheap labour for his business. "Come in, Démì, am I saying your name right?"

Démì nodded.

"I will introduce you to the others at the café," Bruno wiped his hands on the hand towels tucked into the apron around his waist and walked further into the café kitchen, where there were two girls making sandwiches. One was in her mid- to late-twenties and the other was no more than fifteen-years old.

"This is Clara and Etola," Mr Genova said.

That evening, Démì made six pounds.

———

"I saw an advert outside the agency window today for warehouse staff. They pay a bit more per hour," Ernest said.

"What about the meat packing job? Are you thinking of leaving it, my darling?" Grace said.

"It's hard on me. I've not been in that kind of cold before. Yesterday, I didn't thaw until an hour after I got home, even though it's summer now. I think I should look for something else."

"Yes, that's just the British summer, my darling. But, I trust you and whatever decision you think is best," Grace said.

———

Ernest did get the warehouse job so he was in from the cold but Grace could tell he was unhappy. There was nothing she could do.

He was constantly cleaning and fixing things around the house and quoting Proverbs.

Yesterday, she overheard him talking to Démì for hours – Démì couldn't get past the fact that wisdom was a woman.

She really didn't think the semantics of whether or not wisdom was a woman was beneficial to a teenager.

She wondered whether to talk to him. They had heard nothing about any of the sales and marketing jobs he had applied for.

Ernest left the job at McDonald's and was now helping their friends the Cokers to clean a school. So, on his days off or whenever he had morning shifts at the warehouse job, he helped Olú and Alice Coker in the evenings to clean the school in Slough.

Grace was happy because it meant extra money for food and they could pay for school trips for the children but she rarely saw her husband and when she did, he was tired.

"I sent Yẹyè some money today," Ernest said to Grace one Saturday afternoon.

Knowing what a money pit Ernest's sister could be, Grace adjusted herself in her seat and picked her words carefully. "What did she need it for?"

"Well, she wants to start a new business, you know, start working for herself. Sewing clothes or something like that plus one of her sons is in trouble with the law and they told her to bring some money to exonerate him." Ernest could feel Grace getting tense next to him. He understood it was a great strain for the family at the moment but what was he supposed to do when his relatives asked for his help? Luckily or unluckily, Grace's brothers never asked her for money because they thought she was just a woman although they never failed to drop big hints to Ernest, to which he always responded, 'I need to ask my wife'.

"Didn't you send her money last week?" said Grace.

"That was two weeks ago," said Ernest.

"Ok, we just have to make sure when your sisters ask for money that we are being careful. I mean sometimes what we send them is a day's wages and we can't let them think it is so easy to get that money."

"I know, thank you," said Ernest and he kissed her.

———

"What are you eating?" Chloe said, approaching Ìní who was sitting alone in the cafeteria. Katie followed closely behind her carrying a tray.

Oh God, here they come again. To question me on my food choices. But that's the thing, they aren't choices. I just eat whatever my Mum puts in here. That's why I'm always eating these things you call weird. It's leftovers from last night. Guess what? It's weird to me you eat dry food placed between bits of dry bread. Please let me eat my food in peace.

"It's Nigerian food," Ìní said curtly to dissuade further queries.

"It's weird. Why is it that colour?" Katie piped up. She loomed closer to examine the contents of Ìní's lunch box.

"I don't know why it's that colour. It's from cassava."

"What's cassava?"

"It's like yam, from the potato family."

"Potato family," Chloe and Katie repeated and erupted into laughter. Then carrying their tray, they walked off to sit at another table.

———

That afternoon, Ìní had stern words with her mother about the contents of their lunch box.

"Mummy, why can't we have sandwiches in our lunch box like the other children in school?"

"Why, what's wrong with what I gave you?"

"The kids at school were making fun of me today. They said my food was weird!"

"Me too!" Démì piped up.

"Weird, what's weird? That's all we can afford. I'll buy some sandwich stuff next week. Your father didn't get paid this week so we don't have money for crisps and ham. If those kids make fun of you, report them to the teacher and if they don't stop, I'll come to the school myself."

Démì and Ìní looked at each other, knowing that was not a workable solution. Still, they took garri to school every day for the rest of that week. Ìní found an empty classroom to eat alone and Démì told anyone who asked about his food, that it was all they could afford and, in the process, offered them some.

———

"Démọlá, come!"

Ernest was washing the car. "How's it going in school?" Ernest finally said after Démì had been standing there for close to ten minutes.

It was chilly and Démì had started to feel the chill through his favourite shirt, now worn thin from overuse. Sensing one of his long lectures about Proverbs, Démì tried to keep it brief. He knew his father could be verbose and apart from the cold, he wanted to get back to watching the Premiership match.

"It's going well, sir."

"Going well. What does that mean? How is your class? How are your teachers? Do you need extra coaching for your GCE?"

"It's GCSE, Dad."

"Ehn, it's GCSE. What did I just say?"

"It's going well. I don't need extra coaching, sir." Knowing his father would soon depart for his night shift at the hospital. Ernest was now working full time at a private clinic, a job he got through Dr Elson, one of the doctors that worked with Grace. It paid very well and the children noticed things seemed to have settled down between their parents, the whispered conversations and Ernest's stress-induced cleaning had calmed down a bit.

Démì changed the topic, "When are you going to work?"

"I leave in thirty minutes, right after dinner."

"Dad, can I go and finish helping Mum in the kitchen?"

"Yes, ok go," shaking his head, Ernest muttered, "these kids are getting insubordinate, they were not like this back home."

Chapter 8

The Àlejòs had moved to Cavendish Court, a new development nestled at the edge of Windsor, in the corridor leading into Dedworth. They had been living there for six months and while the family felt lucky to have moved out of Grace's cramped hospital-owned apartment, the atmosphere on the council estate was less than palatable. To leave the house was sometimes an endeavour because the kids on the estate were always waiting to abuse and denigrate them.

"Did… you see them… writing the graffiti?" The policeman was a slow speaker, like he considered every word. His patterns of speech came out in short bursts of two to three words, like he measured then dished them out.

"No, but when we were scrubbing it off, a few of them came over, laughing and saying they did it but we'll never catch them," said Ernest.

"Did you… recognise which… who they were?"

"No, but my son did. He's the one that saw and heard them." Ernest turned and yelled in the direction of the stairs, "Démì, come here!"

"Yes, Daddy," Démì came down the stairs and stood by the door, staring at the two officers.

"Tell the policeman what happened when you and Ìní were cleaning the graffiti."

"When my sister and I were cleaning the wall, she went inside to get more soap and one of the boys came over, I recognised him from around the estate and he started laughing and said, 'You'll never find out who wrote that'. I said, 'What did you say?' He said, 'I said it was me' and he laughed some more. I started screaming at him and that was when Dad and Mum came out the door.

"Look sir, I'm sorry… about what er… happened to your family… regarding the er… racist graffiti. Like you said… you've got it… cleaned off now. If… you see… anything else… give us a call."

"It's not the first time. You never do anything. This isn't the first time they've defaced our property with racist graffiti or they've shouted abuse at us as we're walking past or the time they threw stones at my car on my way to work and broke my window. Your colleagues came and didn't do anything then either."

"Look sir, we can't do anything unless you have evidence and you catch them in the act," the other officer said. She had not said anything so far.

"Maybe we should buy a camcorder and then I can record it for you," Ernest said.

"We can't afford a camcorder," Grace added gently placing both hands on Ernest's shoulder to imbue him with her calmness. "Thank you for coming," she said to the officers.

Ìní was thirteen and was starting to feel self-conscious about her looks. She had exaggerated facial features that she was still growing into, with long slim limbs that made her look slightly awkward when she walked. She had wide and big brown eyes, set into high cheekbones and a left dimple that showed when she was embarrassed, which was often.

Grace had been doing Ìní's hair weekly and teaching her how to care for it until one afternoon when an errant prong from the parter comb cut into Ìní's scalp, while Grace was carefully sculpting a middle parting. A flinch from Ìní caused such a commotion that the parter comb dug deeper into her scalp.

"Aaaahhhh Mum! What are you doing? Pay attention!"

"Who are you talking to like that? I'm not one of your classmates. Have some respect!" Grace dropped the parter comb in annoyance.

Still hurting from the comb digging into her skull, Ìní was unrepentant and yelled further.

"Fine, you do your own hair!" Grace said and got up from the mini stool.

"Mum, please. I'm sorry," But it was too late. Grace was now thoroughly annoyed and had walked into the other room to join Ernest on the sofa. He was reading a newspaper.

"What happened? He said not looking up. Ìní had been stressed lately and was yelling at everyone. Even her tolerance was low for Démì, whom she usually adored and had all the time in the world for. A few days ago, he'd caught her, with her head in a book, but it seemed she had been crying behind it. When he'd asked her, her response was a curt 'no' and then she'd walked into the other room clutching something in her other hand. He was not used to these teenage behaviours and it was times like these when he wondered if they did the right thing in bringing them into this country.

He stretched his hand and put it on Grace's thigh to calm her slightly. That always seemed to work. She shifted to face him but didn't say anything. Eventually her breathing evened out and she started to read the paper over his shoulder. He angled it so she could see it better and left his hand on her thigh, stroking it gently for her comfort.

———

On Monday morning, Ìní's hair looked like something that could only be described as a multi-highway flyover. She had braided it herself. It had so many criss-crossing braids that it looked like she had required three hands to do it.

Saying nothing, Ernest closed the house door as he escorted both her and Démì halfway to their schools and then turned to take the bus to work.

Later that night, he approached Ìní and asked about her argument with Grace.

"She wouldn't let me have the hair style that I wanted and she dug the comb into the back of my head. I don't think she was paying attention," Ìní explained.

"Don't talk about your mother like that, you know everything she does, she does for you," Ernest reprimanded.

"You asked me what happened," Ìní retorted, now in a gentler voice.

“Maybe I can take you to Slough to have it braided properly?” Grace had lately discovered some black hair salons in Slough, which she had been going to instead of to Peckham.

“Thanks Dad,” Ìní smiled gratefully. Then thinking about the last time he’d got involved in her hair, she added, “I hope it won’t be like the last time when you cut off all my hair.”

Hurt by the accusation in her voice, Ernest said, “Which time was that?”

“The time Démì and I had the same haircut for about a year and everyone laughed at me in school.”

“You didn’t tell me that. Who laughed at you in school?”

Backing down from the accusatory tone in her voice from seeing her father’s hurt look, she explained. “Well, Aunt Yẹyè said because Mum wasn’t around, you couldn’t be bothered to style my hair weekly so you buzzed it all off and made me look like a boy.”

“That’s not what happened. It’s because every time I brushed it, you would cry and I couldn’t bear to see you cry anymore.” Still distressed by her accusation, Ernest said, “I’m sorry. I realised too late you didn’t like it and I should have asked you first.”

“It’s ok, Dad,” she hugged him and the middle of her head came up to his chin, which made him look down at the mess she’d made of the crisscrossing braids.

“From now on, I’ll take you to Slough to get it done. Let your mother rest on Saturdays. She works nights.”

———

Fanning himself in the dense cloud of the heat wave, Ernest said, "We took a gamble."

"Yes, you took a gamble and looks like it paid off," Dalos spread his arms expansively. "You have a nice house, I mean your place is really nice, your children are about to go to university. We've had to borrow money extensively to pay for Maria and Goke's education. It's nasty, those loans out there and I've had to start from scratch whereas if I'd listened to you," he said pointing to Grace, "and started ten years ago, I know where I'd be now. My brain would be sharper and I'd pass the medical school exam."

The Tìmáyọ̀s had come to visit the Àlejòs all the way from Essex.

"Hmmm mmm," said Ànú. "We were wrong all those years ago when we told you not to move."

"Listen everything looks easy from the outside but we've made sacrifices too," Ernest said. "Who can say whose choices would've been better in the long run? Don't blame yourselves. I'm just glad to see you didn't get caught up in the political ruckus of the recent election."

"Yeah I heard it was really bad. They were burning houses and things," said Grace.

"Yes, we lost all of the clinic," Ànú added sadly. "So, our livelihood was gone and even though we had our home and the kids, Dalos couldn't work and it was hell for a while."

"I realised then instead of buckling down, I should have left earlier," Dalos said. "These government contracts, while lucrative, once the other party wins, it's over, plus people are waiting in the wings just to burn your house down." He squeezed his hands together at the memory of the pain."

Sensing his discomfort, Grace got up to pour him more tea.

"But we're ok now. Things are looking up. I'm retraining as a health scientist here. So, a lot of skills can be transferred over. I have a lot of contacts from my time here at University of London so they've been helping me pivot." Ànú reached over and held her husband's hand.

"I'm so sorry for what happened to you. Do you think you'll be heading back soon?" said Ernest.

"Never!" Ànú said and squeezed his hand tighter.

"They're such a lovely couple," Grace said.

"Yes," Ernest agreed. "What do you think about all that stuff they said about us making the right choices?"

"I think it's been hard but they are right," Grace answered, knowing her and Ernest had been arguing a lot lately about their choices, him hankering for and romanticising his parallel life back in Nigeria. She was fiddling with pots and pans, careful not to say anything, watching for his response to the whole thing. But he said nothing, so she was quiet too.

After a while, she started making dinner, but she noticed his introspective mood lasted the whole evening and well into the next day. She didn't want to bother him, so when they asked her to do an extra shift at work, she said yes, justifying to herself they needed the money, but really it was to avoid Ernest. She was worried he blamed her for his recent unhappiness and the truth was, she also blamed herself but to look that truth in the eye was to confirm it so she skulked around it, talked around it, anything but confront it.

Ernest on the other hand, was looking for a way out that pointed to freedom. Most days he felt like he was blowing in the wind with no control over where the wind would blow him next but when he looked at his children, he felt proud of what him and Grace had achieved. Ìní was sometimes sad and introspective, but Ernest figured she took after him and she kept getting good grades so it was all probably ok. He did occasionally wonder what she was writing in the notebook she was often clutching and one day, he asked Grace about it.

"She's soulful, like you. Remember when I first met you and you used to write me those notes?"

"Yeah, it was the only way I could express the many thoughts bothering me inside," Ernest said. "It was a lot," he added after a short pause.

"I appreciated them," Grace said.

Getting in and out of the estate had become tough for Ìní, who had become perpetually afraid ever since the estate youths had chased down her father with hockey sticks one evening on his way to work, they had then leaped on his car and shouted racist abuse at him.

The shadow of the event loomed over Ìní, even on days when nothing happened as she walked through the estate. Anticipatory trails of fear ran down her back each time, and remained long after she had reached the junction out of the estate.

Sometimes, she would run into them and they would either shout abuse at her, calling her 'black bitch' or say things like 'go back to Africa'. She tried to talk to Démì about it but it seemed he did not have any problems with them. Apart from saying 'Alright, boss' to him as he walked past, he seemed to have little or no interaction with them. She concluded it was hard to discuss something with someone when they have walked the same line and had a different experience. So, she kept it quiet, figuring she would go to university soon and escape it all.

She also knew her mother was trying to keep things quiet and not keep calling the police to the house since they never took any action. Grace thought it was starting to look bad to have police cars outside their house every few months.

Ìní chose to focus on her studies instead as that seemed to make her parents happy.

"Which courses are you applying for?"

"Literature and maybe something else, I haven't decided what the other thing should be yet," Ìní said.

The guidance counsellor looked at Ìní above her glasses, then took them off, the chain rattling against the frame. She had thinning hair, culminating in an enormous widow's peak and a severe hairline. Perhaps in an attempt to distract from the state of the hair, she had dyed it blonde, which Ìní guessed had not worked out well because in the harsh light of the office, it fluoresced with embers of green. Some of the students called her Miss Beetlejuice which Ìní had always thought a little unfair. Today though, after their interaction, Ìní wondered if such a harsh nickname had not been warranted after all.

"You know, you should probably study something a little more realistic," Mrs Bailey-Whitmore said after a short silence of staring at Ìní, waiting for a different answer from 'literature'. Still that was all the answer Ìní had, so she kept quiet. She didn't have a back-up plan.

"Which universities are you applying to?" said Mrs Bailey-Whitmore finally.

"I've made a shortlist based on the top twenty in the league table and distance from home," said Ìní.

"Hmmm..." Mrs Bailey-Whitmore grunted, then started laughing.

Ìní was confused. *Why was she laughing?* She waited until the laughter had finished then said, "Miss, do you think it's a bad idea?"

"I just don't want you to be disappointed," Mrs Bailey-Whitmore said, then started rooting around in her drawer to pull out a printed version of *The Times Good University Guide*. She put her glasses back on and pointed to universities near the bottom. She turned the paper over to Ìní and said, "I don't think you'll have any trouble getting into these ones. These will accept you."

"Which university did you go to, Miss?"

After a short pause, Mrs Bailey-Whitmore said, "I didn't go to university. But that's not the point. My job is to advise students and I think these will be the best choices for you. Aim for universities in the range of seventy and below." She pointed helpfully to the universities she meant, which Ìní did not recognise. She simply had not looked there. Her grades were good so she had assumed she would be able to aim higher in the league.

For the rest of the day, what Mrs Bailey-Whitmore said stayed with her. *These teachers have a lot of students and they graduate many per year so she must see patterns and know some things*, Ìní thought. *But she must also know my predicted grades, that I meet the requirements of those universities I am aiming for? Maybe she is mixing me up with someone else.*

As she walked home later that day, she mulled over what Mrs Bailey-Whitmore said. By the time she reached the threshold of the house, she had discarded it all. *Stupid Miss Beetlejuice.*

———

"Ìní, oya come,"

"Yes, Daddy,"

"What are you going to study for higher education?"

"You mean uni?"

"What did I say? Higher education and university? Is it not the same? Your mouth like uni."

"I was thinking of studying literature," said Ìní.

"What is literature?" said Grace.

"English literature," said Ìní.

"What do you think about Economics?" said Ernest. "Dr Tìmáyọ̀'s first born is studying that in Wolverhampton and after his graduation, he's got a good job lined up in Birmingham. He's doing well. Very well.

You should study the same. They say you are guaranteed a good job."

"Good job, Ìní," Grace buttressed.

"But you told me they also told you not to come here, not to educate us here and it was the worst advice you'd never taken," Ìní said.

"You know your mother and I worry about our efforts in this country. I did not come all the way to this country for you to go and study English literature. Literature kẹ̀? Kí lo fẹ́ fi ṣe? What are you going to do with it? You know what happened to all the people I knew back home who studied literature? They're working at petrol stations selling oil. They're nobodies today," Ernest's leg shook with the intensity of his lecture and he started shaking his head.

Ìní was constantly writing in a little notebook she carried everywhere. Démì approached her one Saturday afternoon mid-scrawl, he needed help with an essay for his English class. He had lost a year when the family moved to England because they had put him in the class year above her, instead of two years, which had demotivated him somewhat. He needed to write a story that was personal to him, so he asked to borrow one of Ìní's stories in exchange for doing her maths homework for two weeks. Deal, she said and asked for a Galaxy bar on top. Démì now had a Saturday job, so he was starting to have a bit of money, which sometimes made him unbearable but he was generous when he wasn't busy spending it on his secret girlfriend. Ìní pretended she didn't know about her, to not get him in trouble with their parents. She knew what their reaction would be, "Did you come to England to find a girlfriend or face your studies?"

So, she wrote him a new essay, she didn't want to share one of the written ones from her notebook. Démì on the other hand, submitted it without reading it, until he was asked to read an excerpt in class. It was a tale about everybody needing to be protected sometimes. It ended in a little ditty, which stuck with Démì for years. It opened a keyhole into Ìní's private world. He had no idea what his little sister had been going through.

Maybe we can hide in the trees
Like the Egret or the Leopard,
The enemy never looks up
And we can look down
Birds in trees
Cannot be hurt
When trouble comes
Wrap me in trees

Part 3, 1975

Chapter 9
Ibadan, Ọ̀yọ́ State, Nigeria

Theirs was a love of surprises. Grace was surprised by Ernest's gentle, open manner and he was surprised by how fast he fell for her.

Grace had gone to the UAC that morning to get pots and pans after moving into a new place on Òdólẹ̀ street in Ibadan, and finding that furnished meant a sofa and an inordinate number of stools and nothing else.

She had pondered long and hard about how to prioritise spending her salary advance. *Food or bed?*

She'd decided food. *I will sleep on the floor until I can afford a bed.* The store was close to the hospital, which meant she could carry her spoils home without needing a taxi.

"Hello, can I help you?" A tall man with a wide smile and a neatly hedged afro was looking at her and smiling.

Ernest looked Grace right in her eyes. Immediately she was disarmed. She was used to how men treated her in these parts especially if she was wearing her nurses' uniform. They were dismissive and never quite made eye contact, they either talked down to her or asked where her husband was before they would serve her.

"Yes, I need to buy some pans, please?"

"Let me show you."

He took her to the second floor and there, next to the refrigerators, were the pans. She saw the prices first before she saw the pans. Grace hesitated, she couldn't turn back without alerting the gentleman that actually she could not afford this place.

He turned to lean on a fridge. His crisp white shirt clashed wonderfully against his even brown skin. He smiled and he had teeth so white and straight that she found it distracting for a minute. Again, he kept eye contact. Something about the way he looked at her made her feel respected, like she was something. She wasn't used to that reaction from men, not unless they were younger and societal courtesy demanded it.

"How many pots would you like, ma?"

"Ah... do you have cheaper...?" she looked down, embarrassed.

Catching her meaning, he added, "Look, the market is a much better place to buy pots."

"Oh, but it is far. My place is nearby and I don't want to take a taxi there."

"Oh, you don't have a car?"

"I can't afford a car, I'm just a nurse."

"Just a nurse," he laughed. "Don't say that o! At least two of my sisters tried to get into nursing and failed, so it's not so easy." They both laughed. "Look I can drive you to get the pots. This place is expensive and it's the same quality down at the market."

She looked unsure. *These city guys and their offers of help usually came with strings attached.* She looked away for a moment thinking of what to say to get out of it.

"I can bring my friend along or you can bring your friend if you're not sure whether to go with me. After all, we don't know each other. But you seem like you need help," Ernest said.

"Ok I'll ask my friend. I need it very soon. I have no pots in the house and nothing to cook with tonight."

"Ok I finish at four," he said patting his afro thoughtfully.

Grace noticed his afro edges were trimmed in a perfectly round shape, to frame his prominent forehead which suited his big brown eyes very well. *He's very handsome*, she thought.

"How about you come back here with your friend and I will pick you both up from the front of the building?" Ernest said.

She walked the fifteen minutes back to the hospital to ask Lànà if she could escort her to get some housing supplies with a strange man she had just met. Lànà, was dubious that this man only wanted to help her to just buy pots, but agreed to go with them after her shift.

Ernest was perfectly behaved on their shopping trip, he helped Grace to buy some other housing supplies she needed, haggling with the market women, whom he seemed to know quite well. They kept calling him, 'Oga UAC' and some of them called him, 'Son'. She also noticed his reciprocal reverence for them. On his good will with them, she managed to get more stuff on hire purchase with the promise to pay back at month's end when she got her salary.

Ernest helped her to furnish the apartment with his other discounts with various retailers in the Ibadan province. Turned out he had lived in Ibadan for about five years after his father abandoned them and his sisters dropped out from school. He wasn't married because he was helping to put his sisters through school, being a huge proponent of education like her.

She found that he talked too much but she also liked how he was an open book. Although a reserved person herself, Grace appreciated his verbose nature and felt that she could trust him.

They didn't start dating for another year. He seemed content with their friendship and had other focuses besides work. He was a good spender, choosing to send his money back home to his mother and sisters for their education rather than drinking and partying like the other young guys she knew.

Once when a doctor at work asked her out and she told him to see his reaction. Rather than being jealous like she expected, he'd said gently, "Make sure he's not already married. Polygamy can cause problems. I saw what it did to my parents."

He'd said no more than that and carried on driving.

After Ernest first helped Grace with stocking her house with white goods, he hadn't had the courage to ask for her landline so he'd said an awkward goodbye and left her standing holding the door. Grace, equally lacking in confidence, had said nothing and let him leave.

The next time she saw him was at church. Ernest, not normally a church goer, had found out where the nurses worshipped and had gone there to look for Grace. It took him three Sundays to find her.

When she saw him, he was wearing a crisp blue dashiki with gold embroidery and matching trousers. In his enthusiasm when preparing, he had overused starch, such that the sleeves on his dashiki were so sharp that it kept cutting into things.

"Grace!"

She had seen him from the balcony earlier in the service but she took a moment and paused before she answered. He called again and she turned around.

"How are you?" he said softly, hesitantly.

"Good. Thanks again for your help the other week. How is work?"

"Good. I was thinking of you. We have some kettles now. They're driving out the old stock and with my discount, I thought maybe you could come by and get some."

He couldn't believe he was talking about kettles when what he really wanted to do was to ask her to go for dinner. He had been planning his speech for three weeks but in the cold light of the day and the piercing brightness of her clever almond-shaped eyes, he lost his nerve. She was so quiet, she had a way of looking through you, such that you felt she knew everything you were about to say. Yet there was a kindness and gentleness in her manner that drew him in. He found that any time he spent in her company left him feeling calm and capable, like he could do anything. He wanted more of that, more of her. But she was hard to read, so he frequently lost his nerve around her. As a salesman, he never lost his nerve, his livelihood depended on it and there was not a soul he couldn't strike up a conversation with, let alone persuade to buy the overpriced stuff at the UAC.

But standing in front of Grace, he felt unsure of himself.

He didn't have his company car that afternoon, so he had brought his motorcycle.

Later, he took her on his motorcycle and they went for Àkàrà, the roadside beancakes that was popular among couples on dates on Sunday afternoon and evenings. It was busy there so they sat on a fallen oak branch and chatted until the throng of people died down. They talked of family. She talked of her unusual education at the hands of Auntie Winnie, who had sadly now passed away and even though she didn't have a teacher's licence, it hadn't stopped her from educating the neighbourhood girls.

Ernest told her of his four sisters, who had suffered the same fate of lack of education, and remained mostly illiterate. They had married early, thinking it was their only option.

Grace liked the way he spoke of his future plans without hesitation or secrecy. He was very clear about wanting girls and his plans to educate them to the same level if he had boys as well.

She appreciated his openness, being quite taciturn and sometimes secretive herself.

They became friends and would spend Sunday evenings together either getting Àkàrà or going to some other food-related event.

The months when Ernest made a lot of money from his sales job, he would take her to a restaurant.

But all the while he didn't make a move. He just assumed it was a done deal and she was his girlfriend.

One day, Ernest invited Grace to a house party at his. One of his friends was back from America and they were celebrating the new release by *Earth, Wind and Fire*.

Upon arriving at the house, a woman who Grace didn't recognise, but later turned out to be Simon's girlfriend, answered the door. Assuming Grace was a rival, Simon's girlfriend didn't open the door but instead called Ernest down. Ernest, not hearing her above the din of the disco music, took his sweet time to come down because his usually perfectly coiffed afro had collapsed at the back due to too much pomade in one spot. Eventually, unable to revive it, he put an afro pic in there to disguise the crater.

At last, he heard the doorbell again and came down.

Seeing Grace at the door, he got excited and kissed her full on the mouth. He had been thinking about it all day and wondering if she would make it to the party. He surprised himself with his forwardness, so he stepped back and waited for a reaction.

Equally taken aback, but more welcoming of the kiss, Grace wrapped her arms around his neck and kissed him back.

They did not go back inside the whole evening. Instead they sat to the left of the veranda and talked.

"What about Dr Àkàndé?" he asked her in the course of the evening. "Are you two together? You know how I feel about these things?" He was asking about the doctor who had been after Grace at the hospital.

"No, we're not together. He has a girlfriend back in his home town."

———

Unbeknownst to Ernest, Grace was being courted by another doctor from her village, who was keen to make her his second wife. Grace didn't take him seriously so she didn't mention it to Ernest but her family liked the doc and wanted her to marry him.

He had promised the moon and stars in dowry and Grace's mum in the village had all but given her consent.

This avoidance tactic precipitated in a showdown one Friday afternoon when Ernest came to wait for Grace at home towards the end of her shift.

There was a white Mercedes in front of the house, with a driver sitting in front and a large man in a white agbádá and cap sitting in the owner's corner looking resplendently smug. Both men assumed the other had come to see Lànà.

Grace approached the house wearing her uniform. "Ìyàwó mi," the large man greeted Grace with a warm kiss on her forehead. She curtsied to greet him.

"Good afternoon, sir," Grace said.

Ernest was confused. *Who was this guy? Ìyàwó mi? Why was this guy calling Grace his wife?* The Grace he knew hated such flamboyance and always told him so, when she saw the big men about town in Ibadan with their fancy cars and fleet of wives. Besides, this man was already wearing a wedding ring. He tried to keep calm but eventually said, "I'd like you to explain yourself sir what you are doing with my girlfriend?"

"Who is this speaking òyìnbó? Don't you know I'm a medical doctor? You can't confuse me with your English," the doc reached out from under his agbádá and clocked Ernest in the jaw.

Ernest, although not expecting a punch from under the layers of the opulent clothing such as the agbádá, was ready with his own and knocked the man from under the jaw.

After a kerfuffle of punches, which ended when the doc's driver came out to separate them. Grace was crying and sitting in despair on the sidewalk.

The doc said to Ernest, "Ìyàwó wa ni. Her parents have given me their consent."

"Do you have Grace's consent?" said Ernest. "She is my girlfriend and we've been dating. In fact, I want to marry her."

At this, Grace recovered quickly and interjected, "You never said you wanted to marry me."

"I do. Just haven't got up the nerve to ask you yet. Here, here is the ring. I've been carrying it around for months. When you make up your mind, come and find me."

He bent to give Grace the box containing the ring and then rode off on his motorcycle.

"I didn't know you wanted to marry me," Grace said when she went to see Ernest at home the next day.

"It was implied," he said softly, looking down at his interlaced fingers. He moved closer on the sofa and kissed her.

To Grace, it felt like sinking into heaven and she never wanted to come out.

Ernest, having held himself back from this moment for so long, finally felt like he was flying. He held her tenderly and amazed at his restraint, stroked her back simultaneously to calm himself.

The opposing sensation made Grace feel calm and excited at the same time.

———

Grace had had boyfriends before but not like this. He was attentive and generous of spirit in a way that was compelling to be around and she loved him before she even knew how to articulate it.

He also would bring her fruit sometimes when he heard on the news that government salaries had stalled, which often happens when the federal government released funds but it got embezzled at the state level. One such time lasted months so he would bring her rice and oil and other staple foods so she could cope. He also brought some for her roommate, Lànà.

On the months when Ernest's bonus was good, he took Grace out and spoiled her.

Sometimes he would go home to give money to his sisters and these visits would last weeks. In these times, she missed him and wondered why he needed to go home for so long.

Chapter 10

2005, Windsor, Berkshire, UK

"I want us to start thinking about our future," Ernest said one afternoon.

"What do you mean?" Grace said.

"I want to start building a house back home for when we retire."

"My children are here. Where would I go?"

"I'm not saying leave right away but one day these children will move out, I want to go back home. I can't be a cleaner forever."

"I thought you liked that job, they leave you alone there. Dr Elson said you were really getting along there," Grace said.

"Yes, it is true. There is something to be said for a private clinic. It is spotless there and honestly there isn't that much to do. Sometimes, maybe some Botox drips on the floor, that's it, or on a really bad day, someone will forget to hang the laser stick back up on the handle and I have to put it back. But Grace this is not my dream. Maybe you are living your dream and working as a nurse, but my dream was to own a bookshop and I gave that up for us. It's been seven years that I've been in this country. I need to know there's an endgame. I want to go back home."

"Ọkọ mi, but what will I do back home? I would have to start again there. Most of my connections have left or are retired. My pension is here. What will I do?"

"We will find something to do. Ṣebí it's our home. We will find something but I cannot stay here for much longer. It is cold and these kids are grown. It is time to go home. Besides, Simon has been talking to me about some contracts back home."

At the mention of Simon, Grace folded herself further into the couch and looked out the window. Without any more eye contact, Ernest knew Grace was done with the conversation, he got up to get himself a drink.

Ernest had begun to feel a frustration curl up on the inside of him that refused to budge. It was worse in the mornings, knowing he'd have to work again. He couldn't unravel it, it was stodgy and when he tested it with his mind, he felt like he was looking into an abyss. Sometimes he wondered if it was possible to explode from the frustration. It had congealed into a solid mass on the inside of him that sometimes he would forget to breathe.

The trouble was, every time his mind examined it, it grew. When something happened, an argument with Grace or with a colleague, it grew.

With time, his frustration turned to indifference and he stopped talking. First, to Grace and then to the children. The children were too busy to notice what was going on with their usually loving, jovial father. Grace took more night shifts at the hospital to get away from the silence.

Part 4, 2010

Chapter 11
London, UK

Mia distinctly remembered the day she met Démì. He wore a light-blue shirt. It reminded her of gathered clouds. She couldn't tell if it was the deliberate pattern of the shirt or the fading patches of a beloved old blue shirt.

As he approached her, he turned to his right and she took her left. They were both heading for the lift. She complimented him on the shirt. He looked at her, surprised. She noticed he was much younger than he impressed. There seemed to be more than a moment before he eventually acknowledged the compliment.

After that, she saw him everywhere.

Eventually, after the office Christmas party, he asked her out.

After that, they were inseparable.

———

"Good afternoon, can we get a table for two, please?"

The waiter looked him up and down. Démì had been here before and had been too intimidated to ask for a table. He'd left with his tail between his legs.

"A table?" the waiter said after staring at Démì for what felt like an age.

"Yes, a table." Démì looked around. The place was near-empty which was not odd for Monday lunchtime. *Why was this man behaving strangely? Wasn't it his job to allocate a table?*

"For how many people?"

"Two, please."

"Are you with anyone?"

"Yes, he's on his way."

"Ah, Démì, there you are!"

Démì turned around to see his boss behind him. As soon as the waiter saw Mr Pendleton, he smiled and said, "Good afternoon, Mr Pendleton, please follow me, your usual table is this way."

Démì filed the incident under uncomfortable. Yet, he noticed he got the same treatment every time he went there with Mia but not with one of his other colleagues from the law firm.

One day he was relaying the story to a friend, who said, "Why don't you stop going there?"

"They simply have the best steak this side of the river," Démì said.

———

"So, what was it like having your mum away for so long at that age?"

"I just remember the rushed phone calls. There were no mobile phones back then, of course. The tininess of her voice, like she was stuck down a well," Démì looked down, and picked at his palms on the table. Mia reached out to grab them but he pulled away slightly, he didn't like being this vulnerable. Later, he brought his hands back and gripped both of hers across the table. A moment passed, then a waiter came to the table to refill their glasses and they disconnected their hands.

"Sometimes I'd get images of fishing her out of a well…" Démì scratched his chin slightly like he was trying to concentrate. His stubble made a sandpaper-like noise, which he knew Mia liked. She looked up at him, waiting for him to continue. "The phones were old. It was our neighbour's, so they would come and call us whenever Mum called. I had to listen intently, which sometimes made me tired. I was seven or eight, so I would feel guilty about not wanting to talk to her sometimes. Not much was actually said though, except pleasantries because it was so expensive. Afterwards, I'd be left with this mixed feeling. It was part confusion. Part unexhibited joy. Dad would get super introspective afterwards. That part was hard… hard to decipher."

"That must have been difficult having these private family moments in front of strangers?" said Mia.

"Actually, the hardest part was that you had to rush through anything you wanted to say. You didn't want to be the one who exhausted the whole airtime her coins had paid for. Ah, that dreaded ping sound." Démì grabbed his face in frustration. "It never happened on my watch, of course, but the fear was always there."

When Démì dropped Mia off that night, he sat and thought about having walked those old memory lanes. His senses had felt it so keenly, such that he felt transplanted for hours afterwards, like he was reliving it.

He realised he'd never talked about it before. He did not sleep well that night.

Démì and Mia had taken to arguing a lot about code-switching. He complained that she was different around their colleagues than when she was alone with him, and she hated the way he complained his career wasn't progressing when she knew if he just tried a little bit more to play the game and blended in, he would progress. They were at an impasse. One day after a football game, Arsenal had lost, Démì was hankering for a fight with Mia and he got one.

"Why don't you ever tell people that you're from Ghana?" he said suddenly, getting up from the front of the TV and finishing his beer.

Mia was cutting up vegetables for a stir-fry. She dropped the knife and looked round at him in surprise. "Because it never comes up. Because that's not just what I'm about. I've also lived in Amsterdam and honestly being Ghanaian is not the most interesting thing about me."

"It's not the most interesting but it does explain eighty percent of your behaviour."

"Says who?"

"Says the fact that it's not a party for you unless there's jollof rice. The fact that you're not truly happy unless a meal has plantain on the side and you're smacking your lips to Malt," said Démì.

"Those things are true for you too and you're not Ghanaian! What's brought this up anyway?"

"Well, yesterday at work, I noticed you changed your accent when that colleague approached us mid-conversation."

"And?"

"It just bothered me, that's all," Démì shrugged.

"It's called survival, Démì! I'm not from here. I do whatever I have to do to fit in. If that means changing my accent when I'm talking to my boyfriend at work, who by the way, people don't gossip about that he's dating a colleague, only about me, Démì."

"Are you saying things are easier for me there?"

"Yes, because you're a man. You have certain advantages. People assume competence before they meet you. It is unfair of you to accuse me of these things when you enjoy those advantages!"

"What advantages? I also face racism, like in that steak restaurant I'm always taking you to, they treat me differently when I'm with Mr Pendleton than when I go with you."

"But the point is you go with Mr Pendleton. I've never been invited to go with the boys and I've been at the firm longer than you. When discussions about promotions are made at the gym locker room, I'm not there. And, by the way, I hate that steak place!"

"You hate the steak place, why didn't you say? I just want you to be yourself that's all. It's embarrassing."

"I'm sorry I embarrass you with my survival skills." With that, she grabbed her bag and stormed out of the flat.

Démì watched her out the window as she hurriedly crossed the street towards Finchley tube station. Seemingly remembering she had driven to Démì's earlier, she walked back more slowly to retrieve her car. She dropped the keys several times before she finally got the car open.

Démì sat exasperated on the sofa. When he had calmed down and the glaze of anger had lifted from his eyes, he realised he had taken his frustrations with his job and his team losing out on her. Yet he couldn't shake the sense of betrayal he felt by her code-switching.

As time went by, Démì realised he was not that happy anymore. He felt split working at the law firm, like he was now running two distinct personalities and they were not in continuum.

He found that when he swallowed his words and personality at the firm, he got better projects but when he was talking about issues that affected his community or things close to his heart, he felt side-lined.

On one spring day in March, he was looking at a website that repatriated people back to Africa. It was in his lunch hour, in between writing a contract for a particularly difficult client. By the time, he looked at his watch again, it was 4 p.m. He realised he must have been looking for more than two hours. The next day, he looked again and for the next month, he looked some more. By the end of June, he had applied for a couple of jobs. He did not tell Mia.

Leaving Mia was a surprisingly easy decision for Démì to make. He blamed her for all his visceral cultural discomfort and believed everything would be better if he could just get back to Àkúrẹ́. He had heard rumblings through Ìní that their dad might be moving back too but he knew his parents were joined at the hip and his Dad would never actually take the plunge.

No matter.

He was leaving and that was it. He was so happy when he finally made that decision. He remembered the day he decided. He'd had a tough day at work and another argument with Mia. He looked at his savings and figured he could survive about eight months without a job.

The economy wasn't particularly joyous and with the recession still digging its heels in, he had heard of a few people moving back to Africa after the 2008 financial crash to start again doing various bits in business, mostly in tech. He would try his luck too.

He told his dad who was surprisingly positive and Démì supposed that was what convinced his mum too. She did not raise much of an objection although she was always saying how glad she was they were all together as a family again, after the years she had spent wandering alone. His father had given him some names of people back in Àkúrẹ́ to contact for starting a business.

Telling Mia was easy because she was no longer speaking to him after their last argument. He had tried calling her to no avail and every time he saw her at work, she would dodge him. Eventually, he wrote her an email and he supposed she would've also seen the company-wide announcement that he was moving to Nigeria to pursue other opportunities. After that, he had seen her by the lift and she had refused to make eye contact. She was wearing his favourite dress of hers, the black sheath one with the gold zip running all the way down the back. She turned her back to him and walked the other way when she saw him coming. Her head was raised high but he could tell by her shoulders and wobbling heels that she was slightly rattled at the sight of him. He felt free of a relationship that made him uncomfortable. He was finally happy to go find himself.

That was the last time he saw her before his last day in the office.

She did not reply to his email.

"Is this what you're going to do with your life? Running around with that Ìkẹ́mi girl with the rich parents?" said Grace to Ìní.

Ìní figured it was rhetoric so she did not answer.

Ernest walked in, back from his night shift. He was wearing blue trousers, a black fleece and work boots and a flat cap. He looked tired. His face was worn and his eyes were red. Ìní was moved with compassion at how hard her parents worked. She thought about university. *Had she not tried hard enough?* She tried to attend as many lectures as she could but Economics had not been for her. She did not find it easy to understand the equations and what they were saying. The politics modules were better. She loved the debates and the postulations but everything else was foreign to her.

She had to go back to the coffee shop later tonight. She tried to find a way to excuse herself but Grace's lecture was now in full swing, which must mean Ìní's drifting life must have really been bothering her for a while now. *She doesn't normally speak this much*, Ìní thought.

Ernest leaned against the kitchen cabinet and watched the whole thing. At some point, his eyes closed behind his glasses and Ìní could tell he had fallen asleep.

At the end of her long tirade, Grace dissolved into tears and collapsed against the fridge. Ernest woke up from his sleep-standing and comforted her. At a loss what to do, Ìní left quietly.

———

Ìní didn't exactly remember when she started feeling more comfortable in her skin. It may have had something to do with making friends with Ìkẹ́mi at university – the sharp girl from Lagos with the irreverent humour. They were different as chalk and cheese but they got along so famously, not least because of how Ìkẹ́mi liked mixing her metaphors.

Her first memory of Ìkẹ́mi's bravado was during freshers' week, when she overheard Ìkẹ́mi get into an argument with a final year student about the idiom, 'you've hit the nail on the hair'. Ìkẹ́mi doubled down and said she wasn't wrong, neither of them had a book at hand to check the facts and with the library being twenty minutes away, neither got up and no one won the argument.

The group was split.

One guy offered to call his dad on his Nokia phone, he was the only one with a mobile, a small grey brick that he carried constantly, an emblem of his wealth and insecurity, still it came in handy sometimes for their student-living shenanigans. But his father did not pick up that day.

So convinced and dogged was Ìkẹ́mi that Ìní left the argument thinking, maybe it is 'hit the nail on the hair'.

After that, she seemed to hear the phrase everywhere, as is often the case in these matters, first on a BBC sitcom and then in a lecture theatre. She didn't dare bring it up that Ìkẹ́mi was wrong.

Chapter 12

Démì's heady dreams of returning to Àkúrẹ́ came crashing down with a thud louder than the domestic plane he took from Lagos earlier that morning.

The stale biscuit they gave him on the flight was now playing havoc with his stomach. He was keen to get started with making contacts for his new business. First, he needed to contact Mr Ìshọ̀lá, a man whom Ernest had highly recommended as someone to know if you wanted to do business in Òndó State.

Alas, by the time he got there, Mr Ìshọ̀lá had been transferred to Ọ̀wọ̀. Never mind, Démì thought looking around the empty office. There was a sad desk that served as the waiting area and the bored receptionist in a pale lilac shirt and navy-blue skirt barely looked up at him after rudely announcing to him earlier that Mr Ìshọ̀lá had been transferred.

As Démì drove home in the midday heat, he drove past Ọba Adéṣidà road, the buzzing main street was not what he remembered. In its place were the derelict remains of the once-lively architecture. It felt hollow and so did Démì.

He remembered the old days when it was freshly paved and the buzzing market women sold their bọ̀lè and dùndú on the sides of the streets. The King's market, Ọjà Ọba, lined with the assorted colours of various fruits and vegetables in season: àgbálùmọ̀, mangoes, tomatoes, and various types of fish. Now the street market had been replaced with an arcade and the once-colourful side streets were now a dull umber hue, making Démì's insides twinge in sadness. He longed for the days when his father's bookstore was one of the landmarks on that long commercial stretch of road, filled with sellers of plastics, cold drinks and homewares.

Not wanting to be like all the other diaspora returnees who always ended up moving to Lagos, causing brain drain in some of the other regional cities, he stuck it out for a few more weeks.

I am different and I will move to my hometown, Démì had vowed when he left London. But after a failed attempt to reconnect with some of his father's old cronies, especially Simon who was now in early retirement, had divorced his first wife and was now holed up with two women who were rumoured to be twins, Démì concluded he would have to go to Lagos and figure things out from there.

The first thing Démì noticed when he landed back in Lagos was the ease of moving freely. He realised he didn't have to make his usual split-second adjustments, to make others feel comfortable around him. There were a fair number of internationals in Lagos so he did not stand out much here, except when he spoke and sometimes people turned around. His accent did not match his clothes. Démì had commissioned a tailor to make him a rainbow of dashiki with matching trousers.

His usual microadjustments, both in body and language were gone. When he entered a shop, he simply entered. He didn't worry about whether he had accidentally forgotten to change into a shirt from the hoodie he had worn to the gym. He didn't worry about carrying his shopping basket openly enough, so he didn't attract the attention of the security guard. He needn't smile toothily at the cashier so they wouldn't think he was dangerous and unfriendly. His mind was unburdened by these little worries and it was in the absence of it, that he realised quite how much time these daily niggles took up in his mind and in his body. He supposed that was the freedom of living as part of the majority that some of his friends back in London sometimes took for granted.

His towering height and keen sensory observations as a lawyer had made him acutely aware of people's micro reactions to him and it made him more conscious of his behaviour towards others. The other effect it had was that over the years, it had eroded his space and made him try to appear smaller.

The luxury of now moving freely, especially at night, was not lost on him. He remembered in his neighbourhood in Finchley, when walking home from the tube at night, if someone was walking towards him and there was a streetlight, he would make sure to raise his gaze so they could see him properly and how unthreatening he was. Sometimes, he wished he hadn't inherited Ernest's towering height, it could be a burden sometimes. When he eventually started making friends at university, he was used to people saying to him, 'when I first met you, I thought you were scary', to which he had no response. He didn't have the language to ask exactly what made him scary and they probably didn't have the language to explain either. That was his burden to bear until it wasn't.

Having abandoned the vague idea of doing some sort of business with his savings in Nigeria, Démì decided looking for work as a lawyer was the next best thing. He found that he had more positive reactions in job interviews if he hammed up his British accent, so *that* he did, the rest he would figure out later.

He got tired of Lekki for the artificial sheen and scene of the rich there, he felt like a fraud for living like a rich person in this moneyed part of Lagos so he found a flat in nearby Ikoyi, which had a reputation for old money, nonetheless he felt more comfortable with the less apparent display of wealth there.

He found it absurd that the only way to tell if the electricity had come back on was to look at neighbours who had no generators to see if their light was on. Although 'less affluent' was relative in a neighbourhood like this, and his cognitive dissonance in choosing to live there instead of the more trendy Lekki beach was not lost on him.

Lately though, it seemed like the guy next door had gotten himself a small generator so Démì could no longer tell when the electricity came back.

Now, Démì went outside briefly to tell Sunday, the gateman, let him know when the electricity came back on. He felt like a long bath tonight and he didn't want to waste the generator fuel on the water pump. Démì had taken to two washes a day, he was still not used to the heat and he found that he slept better if one of them was a bath.

She was impossibly trendy with blue cat-eye glasses, a blue blouse with sheer bows and culottes, with her braids skimming the top of her bum and a middle parting that made her beautiful. She talked non-stop, and he wasn't quite sure what she had been talking about when she dropped her fork and had to stop.

"Excuse me, did you say you worked at the newspaper?" she eventually asked him after she had retrieved her fork and chewed on a particularly tough pọ̀nmọ́.

Wondering why she had ordered the pig skin, Démì said, "Er no, I'm a lawyer," then he excused himself from the table. The driver had come in to the restaurant to use the toilet and Démì needed to tell him to get the car ready. He had no idea what the traffic from Lekki to Ikoyi would be like at this hour.

He looked around the restaurant, it reminded him of his favourite one back in Finchley. There were a bunch of white guys in the back celebrating something; occasionally they would erupt into bursts of laughter followed by a birthday song. There was an impossibly large fish in the middle of their table which they were devouring with gusto; the beads of sweat of their foreheads signifying they hadn't had the foresight to bribe the maître'd to sit them next to the air-conditioning unit to stave off the heat from the open kitchen.

Coming back to his seat, Démì looked up, the lights hanging from the ceiling looked like fried noodles, shards of light escaping from the intricacies of the thin cylindrical design to light the dim restaurant.

After cat-eye had finished talking, they left quietly.

He didn't think he would see her again, his side was aching from leaning forward so much to listen to her long diatribes. Now he regretted it, he had taken nothing away from their conversations.

———

His eyes were like slits in the middle of his very dark forehead. He balanced his glasses on his nose.

Ortega was now a brandy-drinking father of two. He drank non-stop and talked about what he called his good island life.

They were talking about Démì's dating life since getting back. Démì was lamenting how money-focused the girls were and how they expected him to buy them gifts constantly.

"Look, you gotta deliver the goods," Ortega said with no sympathy.

"What goods?"

"Whatever they need. Whatever they ask. In turn, they don't give you wahala. They don't ask questions, where you've been, shey you grab?"

"I don't get what you mean," said Démì.

"I mean if you want that particular type of girl, the sophisticate. The one who's been abroad and is educated and can hold her own, they come with certain expectations, you grab? But if you settle them and keep them happy, they let you do what you want."

"Is that what Mrs Ortega is like?"

"Listen, I don't want to talk about my wife. We're having a nice lunch." He took a long swill of his brandy and coughed because some of it had gone down the wrong pipe. After he finished coughing, his phone rang and he picked it up, saying very little and wiggling his eyebrows at Démì. Unclear of his intended meaning, Démì picked up his phone to check his text messages.

After the phone call, Ortega said he had to leave to meet his girlfriend. Leaving no room for Démì to ask questions, he took his keys off the table, left some notes that did not cover his bill and hurried to his car.

Bemused, Démì wondered sadly if he'd ever get used to the open attitude towards cheating in Lagos. He thought about Mia briefly and discarded her from his mind. He was here now and he was going to try to make it work.

That night, he wrote her an email which he promptly deleted. It was too soon and she was probably still mad at him for the way he had left.

Chapter 13

"Grace, I'm moving back," said Ernest.

Grace felt her heart rate rise. An electrical impulse of nervous energy ran through her immediately; it felt like one of her hot flashes. Her hands clammed up in sweat and further ripples of it covered her toes and feet. Her only response to this bombshell was to reach down and take her socks off.

"Grace, I am moving back to Nigeria," Ernest repeated.

"I know. I've known for a while. You are not happy. What can I do? I made you move here. Your children are out of the house now and look at us. We sacrificed everything for them and now we have nothing in common."

"You are right. I'm not happy here," said Ernest, finally relieved breaking the news had been easier than he had anticipated.

"I don't want a stranger living here. I lived alone for so long. I can do it again," said Grace.

With that, she got up and went into Ìní's old bedroom. She had been living there ever since Ìní went off to university.

"It's like it's there within my head and my skin, and it keeps rolling around and around but I don't know how to get it out, you know?" Ìní said.

Ìní sat on the sofa facing Ìkẹ́mi. It was late in the evening. They lived in a flat bought by Ìkẹ́mi's parents near London Bridge.

Ìní had crashed out of university a year before graduation and got a job working at a coffee shop in Borough.

Ìkẹ́mi worked as a lawyer in the city and spent her summers in Abuja with her long-term boyfriend, Ládoyè, whom Ìní had never met.

After Ìní moved in, it was Ìkẹ́mi who convinced her to try writing again. Since then, she had been writing nonstop but had lately hit a wall.

"Then why don't you go to a writing club?" Ìkẹ́mi said.

"Is there such a thing?" Ìní asked.

"There's a club for everything these days, no matter how esoteric. People find each other, plus this is London," she said spreading her arms out wide and smiling.

Ìkẹ́mi got off the sofa and walked into the adjacent kitchen. She opened the fridge and glanced inside contemplatively. There was nothing as usual, they were bad at stocking their fridge.

"Maybe you're right, I'll take a look," Ìní finally said.

"Ok, goodnight. I'll see you tomorrow." Ìkẹ́mi found an old puff-puff from the previous weekend, which she munched on as she made her way to her bedroom.

"Goodnight, Nins," she said.

"Goodnight, Kay."

———

The next day, Ìní found a writing club online after searching for hours. Most seemed to be opportunities for budding writers to gather and complain about how difficult writing was, followed by a lot of coffee and then going home. But she eventually found one that promised silence. They coincidentally had a meeting that evening, she decided to go before she lost her nerve.

It was in London Bridge, so it was near the coffee shop in Borough. It was a nice evening for thinking, so she decided to walk.

———

The leader of the group was most unusual. She wore a long floral skirt, and sat on the chair with both her legs folded in a pretzel, so the skirt flowed to the floor and swept gently as she moved and spoke.

Her slow voice matched her movements, and she spoke in deliberate tones in her lilting New Zealand accent.

She spotted Ìní as a new face and decided to do an introduction rather than launch straight into the writing part.

"My name is Melia, short for Amelia, but if you call me Amelia, I'll set my dogs on you. I am the curator of this writing group and I also own the café downstairs. I set this up five years ago after my first novel was published. I was starting to feel like a one-hit-wonder so

I wanted to get my creative juices flowing again with like-minded people. So that's how TRG started. TRG stands for The Writing Group. We like to joke that the W is silent, but in reality TWG was taken. This is a silent group, so we start writing straight away because we find that if we start with catching up about our weeks, lives and stuff, it is harder to get the writing started. We have two coffee breaks, fifteen minutes each. The dogs bark when fifteen minutes is over, then we write. You can leave anytime, especially if you hit a wall. We all know how that can be. Enjoy!"

———

"What are you writing about?" Ìní said to the guy in the salmon-coloured trousers and white linen shirt during the coffee break. She pushed the button on the machine marked 'cappuccino'.

As the muddy-coloured liquid gushed in reluctant spurts from the plastic spout, she shuddered internally. '*Oh dear*', her brain muttered at the thought of the bad coffee.

"Enable 410 of us by William Tyler Writer."

"So, William, what's it about?"

"It's an epic tale of war and revenge set in Congo in the 1800s. Oh and by the way, my name is not William. I'm Faison."

"Fezon?"

"Fai-son, spelt like Maison but with an F."

"I'm Ìní. It's nice to meet you. So, who is William Tyler Writer?"

"Me," he responded enthusiastically.

"Oh, you mean like a pseudonym…"

"Yes," he said.

"But why a pseudonym?"

"I figured if writer was already a part of my name, it'll be easier for people to remember and a lot of writers are called William…"

She laughed. "Ah really? But why Congo?"

"I was born in Paris but I moved around a lot as a child. Apart from France, Republic of Congo is where I know the most about. So, I wanted to base my stories there."

"Wow, that's interesting."

The dogs barked.

"I thought this was a café during the day? Why is the coffee so bad?" she said in a lowered voice.

"It's a tourist café. Plus, she has good cakes, so I think that's what keeps people coming."

———

At the next TRG meeting, Ìní met Melia's husband, Fẹ́ni.

He came up to her during the second fifteen-minute coffee break.

"Hi, I'm Fẹ́ni." he said with an affected accent.

"Oh, is that Nigerian?"

"Yes, it is Yorùbá, short for Afẹ́nifẹ́re. It roughly translates as someone who wishes you well."

"Cool, I'm Ìní. What are you writing about?"

"I'm not a writer. I'm Melia's husband. We own the café, I sometimes come to the meetings to use the quiet space to do the accounting."

He was a quiet man and wore a loud flowery shirt. Ìní got the distinct sense that he swallowed ninety percent of what he had to say.

Faison walked up and joined them. He had been thinking about Ìní since their last meeting. He liked that she seemed self-assured, which he found calming to be around.

Fẹ́ni could see how enamoured with Ìní, Faison already was. He rarely talked to people let alone walk up to them during the coffee breaks, choosing to drink alone and observing others. There was a stillness between the three of them. It was getting quite awkward because Faison had walked up to them and stood right next to Ìní but didn't say anything.

After a few minutes, Fẹ́ni broke the silence and said, "Do you guys want to come to a book tradeshow on Saturday?"

"I thought that was only for businesses selling things?" Faison said.

"It's more for publishers and agents and anyone in the business side of the industry but often writers go, and some have been known to get signed there. It is where BK Boston got signed," said Fẹ́ni.

Faison and Ìní both decided it was a good enough reason. They agreed to meet him there on Saturday. They were excited to see what a book tradeshow was.

———

"Where's Melia?" Ìní asked.

"She's stopped off to place her order," replied Fẹ́ni without further explanation.

They were sitting at a coveted corner booth at an American-type diner in East London.

They had decided to go for a late dinner after that evening's writing club.

It was an open invite but only Faison, Ìní and another guy joined – Ìní privately referred to him as Poet guy because she could never remember his name.

On their walk to the tube station, sensing he was going down the path of the fifth wheel, Poet guy had excused himself and slinked home.

Later at the corner booth, Melia joined them.

"I get nervous about my food arriving cold so I like to order immediately. Every time I come here with a group, one of the meals is always cold and it's always mine. Sorry, I know the owners so they let me."

Now used to Melia's idiosyncratic ways, Fẹ́ni did not respond.

Faison was his usual nervous self. He stared at the football showing on the TV on the other side of the diner, so he wouldn't have to resuscitate the conversation. It was either that or stare at Ìní and he suspected she was starting to notice.

He couldn't believe his luck ending up here with her, he could get to know her more.

"So how did you guys meet?" Ìní finally asked, cutting the silence.

"We all met at the writing club," Faison said, still staring at the TV.

"Erm, she was talking to us," Fẹ́ni replied kindly.

In her gentle New Zealand lilt, Melia launched into their story.

"We actually met at the embassy on the visa line. When I first came to London, I was working for a non-profit. At first, I was an admin assistant but when they found out I was a qualified nurse back home, they convinced me to start doing field work. My first one was a trip to Kano State in Nigeria so I was at Nigeria house to get a visa."

"...and I was there to renew my passport," Fẹ́ni interjected. "I wanted to go home to see my mum."

"We got chatting on the queue line," Melia passed back the verbal shuttle.

"I thought she was beautiful."

"At first, we didn't see each other for a few months, I was in the field for three months," said Melia.

"Six months," said Fẹ́ni.

"Oh yeah, but it was supposed to be three. It just stretched and stretched," said Melia.

"We stayed in touch and when she got back, we dated for another six and then we got married."

Ìní enjoyed the oscillating nature of their story telling.

Encouraged by the wistful look on Ìní's face and interpreting it as a silent quest for more, Melia continued. "Fẹ́ni was the one who first convinced me to write. He found my journal during our honeymoon."

"Yeah, we went to Dorset," Fẹ́ni said.

"We didn't have much money so we went to Dorset," added Melia.

"It was a horrible B and B, but it was fun and the town we stayed in was so beautiful. I was very inspired so I wrote every day."

"She was always so absorbed in her thoughts and when she wasn't, she was scribbling things down. I thought divorce was imminent," said Fẹ́ni.

"Yeah, one day, I accidentally left my journal on the table and he caught a glimpse of it, he saw that it wasn't a divorce plan. Then he asked me about it. It was so cute, he wanted to make sure that I knew he wasn't trying to snoop. Anyway, from then on, he encouraged me to write and so I did and I did and I did until my first novel got published. With the advance, we started The Book Café. That was five years ago now. Fẹ́ni, in the meantime qualified in accounting so he started doing the books. He took over from the dodgy village accountant who was helping us with it before."

It was a pleasant evening. Faison didn't get to find out more about Ìní, apart from when she briefly told them that her family moved over from Nigeria. Her mother had moved first and then six years later, the rest of the family had joined.

'The part that's unspoken about immigration is how it splits families', was all he could think to add.

———

Looking in the mirror, she placed her hands in her pockets. *What perfectly ergonomic trousers, pencil thin at the ankles with pockets just at the right place for her height*. She moved closer to examine what she thought was a pimple on her chin. *Maybe it was one of those under-the-skin ones*, Ìkẹ́mi thought.

It wasn't.

Just some cakes of powder from applying her products in too much haste earlier. Some flakes of powder now fell on her sheer silk chiffon shirt and she moved back to dust it off.

"Are you listening?" Ìní finally said, watching all this in exasperation while waiting to continue talking about her latest bemusement at Faison's behaviour.

"Yes, you said he then walked away after asking you so you're not sure if he really asked you out. Next time he asks you if you're going for drinks with the class, make it clear you only want to go with him. I mean… when life gives you lemons, make limoncello. You've got to make these things happen for yourself, Ìní," Ìkẹ́mi said, now walking away from the mirror to sit down on the love seat with her legs crossed at the ankles, still staring at the way the navy-blue trousers perfectly skimmed her slim ankles. *It's my best feature*, she concluded internally.

"Did you see that woman looking at us earlier at lunch?" Ìkẹ́mi said, changing the topic.

"What woman?" answered Ìní.

"The white woman opposite us."

"Oh, the one sitting with the guy who kept looking at his watch? Maybe she was looking at your beautiful top and jewellery. I noticed her clock your bag as we walked in," Ìní said.

"No, that's admiration and I know that look," Ìkẹ́mi paused to dust some more make-up flakes off her shirt, "No, this was something else. It wasn't hatred but it was a stare down. I get it too when I walk into posh shops. Some white shop assistants always look at me like that especially on days when I'm looking so fly." She flipped her weave. "It's like she was looking at me like, '*How dare you?*'"

"Yeah I've noticed that look too. Sometimes white people look at me like that too and it's when I walk into a posh place where there aren't usually many black people."

"What do you think that is? It's so uncomfortable and I noticed when I'm in a posh shop in Abuja or Lagos, I don't get those looks. I don't have to adjust myself before I walk in thinking, *who's going to stare me down today?*"

"Well, people are aspirational by nature. It's what the entire mortgage, wedding, you-name-it industry is based on. People aren't used to seeing black people in an aspirational sense so if you look successful, it's like you're disrupting the aspirational food chain, racists feel threatened. It's ok if someone they've been told looks the right way occupies those spaces. But actually, every time you attack the success of a black person because you don't understand it or because it disrupts your vision of what's aspirational, that's racism. You don't have to call us names," said Ìní.

Ìkẹ́mi clicked her fingers as she remembered. "It reminds me of that story you told me about your family being bullied by your racist neighbours for almost ten years. You guys had aspirational ideas, you wanted to go to university, you and Démì were good students and I imagine didn't skip school that much," said Ìkẹ́mi.

Ìní shook her head. "No! My parents would've killed me. Yeah, it's exactly like that," Ìní said.

Ìkẹ́mi got up again to fix her hair in the mirror and then turned around to look in her wardrobe, she pulled out a short leather skirt. "Sometimes it is just because they don't hang out with other black people so they only have a one-dimensional idea of what we're like from what they've seen on TV or what they've been programmed to believe. I had some people like that at my boarding school but I also had others who were more exposed to other cultures and were alright." Ìkẹ́mi was now trying on the skirt on top of her navy-blue trousers to see how it would fit with the chiffon top."

"Exactly. It was very painful though living through it," Ìní said remembering the verse she used to recite to calm her fears as she walked past the estate courtyard every day.

Birds in trees
Cannot be hurt
When trouble comes
Wrap me in trees

Faison raised his hand to scratch his head. He was bemused by the question.

"What made you want to ask me out?" she repeated.

"Well I thought you were beautiful and interesting," he said.

"Ok," Ìní responded.

Faison had approached Ìní by the coffee machine earlier that evening at the book club. He'd been planning what he was going to say but he ended up just blurting out "Are you going out for drinks tonight?"

Fully understanding the unasked question and taking her friend's advice, Ìní said, "Yes, we could go for a drink."

Chapter 14

She ran a natural hair community online and was constantly checking her number of followers.

Everything was about talk of authentic hair, which Démì found absurd when everything else she did was try to be British or American.

Tonight, she was complaining about the expats in diaspora returning for the I-Just-Got-Back season. "These IJGBs think that they're it, me I don't have time o," she twisted her front lock back into place and reached for her glass. Her row of rings glistening under their spot-lit table.

There was now a row of people at the bar spotting emblem-prone designer brands written behind their polo necks, as they displayed themselves at the bar.

Démì looked behind him, it was that couple from the parking lot, now making out noisily.

He had been seeing Abímbọ̀lá for several weeks now and at first, they had connected over their love of authentic things but he rapidly realised her interest was in the commercial value behind what she deemed authentic. If she could sell it to her followers, she thought it worth buying into. He had started to look for the quickest way out of the relationship.

Still, he wondered if he was being too hasty. After all, they had also connected on their plans for the future and their love of family. She was clear about wanting to get married and not just because it made life easier and you got more respect, but also if you happened to get stopped by the police. When they had first met, she had told him, wearing a wedding ring meant the police went easier on you because for all they knew, you were married to a powerful politician.

She was also tired of dating in Lagos and was keen to settle down with the right guy. But all the talk of the right person made him wonder how easy things had been with Mia in retrospect, and how hard he had been on her when she was just doing her best to fit in.

Now unable to fit in, in a place he considered his homeland, after more than a decade away, made him feel displaced in a way he could not quite comprehend or explain.

The irony was not lost on him.

———

"He-llooooo?" Démì said lazily.

"Démọlá! You're still sleeping!"

Démì didn't deny it. He had been up until daybreak at Akárá, the chic nightspot that attracted Lekki boys and expats alike, bloviating about inconsequential politics until sunrise.

"How are your Lagos girls?"

"How did you know I was on a date? She left actually. But I stayed with some new friends I met there until," he paused to look at his nightstand, "until two hours ago."

"Wow. So, you didn't go to church then?"

Démì laughed from his belly at her tone. Only his sister could do an impression of their mum so spot on that it took the sting out of the insult.

"Ha, no. It's a fashion show there. I'm looking for a new church."

"Yes, at the bottom of the ẹmu bottle. Gosh I still can't believe they've made ẹmu chic again. Remember when we were growing up, it was those old men that used to drink it."

"Yes, what we now know as moonshine. No distilling, nothing. They just drank it straight from the tree," said Démì laughing.

"What was the name Dad used to call it when we were growing up?"

"Ogogoro!!" They both said at once, cracking up before Démì, in his drunken haze, accidentally dropped the phone on his chest and hung up.

When Ìní called him back, he sounded a bit more coherent and listened while she relayed to him her difficult conversation with Grace and their parents' disapproval of her friendship with Ìkẹ́mi.

"Well look at it this way, Dad moved with us when he was forty-seven. Forty-seven!" He repeated. "That's hard. It's hard to start again when you've hit your stride and you've got a couple of kids and a business where you're your own boss. They moved because of us. So, I think they just get nervous when they think it's all gonna be for nothing."

"It's alright for you golden boy, you studied law. One of their approved courses."

"Yeah and that was hard. I'd rather have done something artistic," said Démì.

“Like what?” said Ìní with sarcasm.

“I haven’t thought about it yet,” Démì said laughing, knowing she was mocking him.

———

Ìní could tell Faison was even shyer than she was and she’d have to help him to ask her out again. So, every time she saw him at the TRG, she dropped hints about various ideas of what she’d like to do on a date. When he seemed to start to grab too many clues, she’d retreat and let him ruminate on the clues.

During the first coffee break one Thursday at the TRG, he asked what she was doing for the weekend.

“I’m working tomorrow and Saturday. It gets so busy at the weekends at the coffee shop. You know what I’d really like, when I’ve worked two days in a row like that, someone to walk me home.”

At the second coffee break, Faison tried to ask her more questions about the coffee shop and what time she finished. She skirted the questions and instead asked him about his work and his family. She could tell he was getting frustrated and wanted to ask more questions but he was too shy and reserved to flip the conversation back to her. So, she left him wondering and left the conversation early.

The next day at 4 p.m., he came to the coffee shop where she worked. She feigned surprise. He sat in the direction of her eye line and worked on his laptop most of the afternoon. At 6 p.m., she tapped him on the shoulder and said, “Ready to leave?”

“Yes.” He rushed to pack up all his stuff. His laptop did not respond to the shutdown prompt, after clicking a few more times, he closed it and shoved it in his satchel.

When he looked up, his brown eyes were rather big behind his semi-rounded lens; he reminded her of a quintessential university lecturer whenever he wore them. They had brown frames and because of the frequency with which he cleaned them, his liquid brown eyes were always luminous through them. Looking at her, he swept back his thick wiry curly hair with his left hand and reached for the bag containing her leftovers, to help her carry them. She let him, and walked ahead of him into the cool open air.

The next day, he showed up again at the coffee shop, but this time she invited him to the flat, ostensibly for dinner before she remembered they never had any food.

When Ìkẹ́mi came home from work, they ordered pizza and danced to 1990s R&B music, instigated by Ìkẹ́mi, who was a fabulous dancer and in the end they ended up watching her.

After a while, Ìkẹ́mi went to bed. Ìní stayed up with Faison, kissing and then talking until midnight when he had to run off to get the last tube.

———

Ìní found Faison inspiring. It was in the way he believed in her.

"Why do you write, Ìní? What do you want to say?" Faison asked as they sat across from each other late one evening at their favourite bistro.

Ìní was surprised by the question but she found herself excited to answer. "It's like it's under my skin, you know? The thing about a great book is, it leaves a sliver in your skin, an imprint in your mind's eye that you always remember."

Faison nodded rapidly in agreement.

"Why do you write?" she volleyed back to him.

"I have to write."

"What do you mean?"

"I write because I have to. I think deep down if you're a writer, those words will always disturb you until they find a page."

"Hmmm, I know exactly what you mean," said Ìní.

"Plus, I write to walk people through the world of others. Creating stories is about empathy. Art is empathy."

"Do you ever write in French?" Ìní asked.

"Rarely. At this point, I think in English but occasionally if I have to write something deeply emotive, I will write it in French first and then translate it into English. I guess my emotions are still deeply connected to my French side." He laughed quietly, such that his shoulders shook more than the action itself.

They spent the evening talking about writing and sharing stories.

Faison had lived an interesting nomadic life. He was a second-generation French–Congolese. His father had moved to France in the late 1970s and married his mother, a cute button-nosed Parisienne.

“So, I was born in Paris and then shortly after we moved for my father’s job, he was a public health doctor, back to the Congo. Then we lived in Senegal and ended up moving mostly around Francophone Africa for a few years, and in my teens, we settled back in Paris.” Faison took off his glasses and started polishing them, then continued, “after graduation, I moved to Amsterdam and then to London to try to improve my English, and get out from the oppression of being a second-generation immigrant.”

“What do you mean?” Ìní said.

“I mean where you are from, there is always a stereotype of you and you can never get out of it. But I wanted to try other moulds. I find that in London, people just treat me as a Frenchman, not an immigrant or mixed-race Congolese or any of those boxes. I wanted a different life experience from that.”

He asked about her part-time job. He was thinking of getting one too and focusing more on his writing.

“But what about the lab?”

“It is almost impossible to be a part-time researcher in my lab, but if I find something that’s not so… how do you say, tasking? Then I can focus more on my writing.” He pushed back his brown wiry hair, which bounced back resiliently.

Ìní watched him carefully. She loved his little gestures with his glasses and his hair, the way he looked down after extended eye contact and his liquid brown gaze beneath his semi-rounded glasses. She admired his ability to believe in what he could achieve and to pursue it without too many self-doubts.

———

Ìní kept her cards close to her chest when it came to her feelings for Faison but occasionally she would check in with Ìkẹ́mi on any behaviours that puzzled her.

Ìkẹ́mi had an equally puzzling boyfriend so her advice did not necessarily elucidate whatever was going on with Faison that week.

It was their six-month anniversary and he wanted to take her to his favourite restaurant in Mayfair. He insisted they ordered his favourite bottle of Merlot.

Ìní, not normally a wine drinker, fell in love with the full-bodied wine with its very little aftertaste. Surprised by how much she liked its woody smoothness, she drank it quite enthusiastically and on the way to the bus stop, clutching Faison's arm, she declared her love for him quite loudly.

Faison, who as yet had not made any such declarations, mentally recorded her ramblings and regurgitated them back to her the next day on the phone. Embarrassed, Ìní sought comfort with Ìkẹ́mi.

"What does it all mean?" Ìní said, distressed and clutching her head in her hands.

"You have to live with it and see where it goes. Look at me and Ládoyè. He rarely says he loves me but in his own quiet way I know he does. He's quiet and considered and he's a thinker. Did I mention to you he's left-handed?"

"What does that have to do with anything? You know your fetish is really weird. What is this partiality of yours to left-handed men?" Ìní said.

"It's only peripheral. I wouldn't rule out a man for being right-handed," Ìkẹ́mi said.

"Peripheral partiality," said Ìní before they both burst out laughing.

Later that day, Ìní went to see Faison. "I'm very embarrassed about yesterday," Ìní said, wishing she could disappear into the couch.

"Listen until now I had no idea you had such strong feelings for me. You keep it locked up. Even the mysterious have to sometimes eat humble pie, sweetie pie or any kind of oxymoronic pie," Faison said.

"You just like saying oxymoronic because you relish the word 'moron'," said Ìní, now laughing.

"Listen, I'm very interested in adjectives that have no business being adjectives."

After cooking dinner, he mentioned to her he wanted her to meet his friends. Feeling relieved, she agreed and they planned to meet them the following week. They agreed to meet in the basement of a church, it was part crypt, part museum, where young Londoners hung out.

Faison's friends were a group of four guys and one girl. Ìní sat next to one called Mia who he had known from his Amsterdam days.

"Faison said he met you in writing class, what are you writing about?" Mia said.

"Mostly poems, but lately I've been thinking about writing a novel, it's easier to get published that way," said Ìní.

"Yeah, I agree, I was the same too. I used to write poetry and short stories but realised there was more of a market for novels."

"Wow, I didn't know Faison had writer friends. He didn't mention it."

"Well, we don't talk about it much. We met playing tennis actually. When he first moved to Amsterdam, he joined a tennis club to make friends," Mia said.

"Ah I see. So, what's your book about?"

"It's about my father. He moved from Ghana to the Netherlands in the 90s, but he was undocumented and he was never really able to come back home. Anyway, we lost him because he passed away there, the book is about my journey to trace his steps."

"I'm sorry about your father."

"No problem, I never really knew him, except through his letters. He left when I was very young. At first, he was a tourist but then he stayed to make a better life for us, and I mean he did but he paid with his life."

"Yeah, often people don't realise it. The high price immigrants have to pay. From the outside, it looks different. My family is from Nigeria and I wouldn't be who I am today if they hadn't left. Leave or stay, either way it's not easy."

"Hmmm mmm," Mia agreed. "The money my father left, mostly under his mattress…" Mia chuckled, but it was a sad sort of mirth, "…is what I used to travel and then eventually move to London."

"What is your book called?" Ìní asked.

"*Kofi.*"

"Yeah, I think I've seen that on the shelves. I thought it was an autobiography of a famous Kofi. I'll be sure to pick up a copy now that I know it's from you. Gosh, I can't believe Faison has never told me."

"It is kind of a biography but it's more of his journey. Why he left, why he stayed away, who he met while there and all the questions I had after he died. I really felt abandoned for a long time until I traced his journey, then I saw things through his eyes, why he made the choices he made."

Later that night, on the walk home, Faison held Ìní's hand. She was touched by Mia's story. She couldn't wait to read her book.

Faison's nervousness was at an all-time low, he was finally glad she had met his friends and they had tacitly let him know she passed the bar of approval. On the way home, he turned to her and said, "Ìní, I never thought I'd meet anyone as dynamic and lovely as you. I feel so comfortable with you and no matter how long we spend together, I'm still excited to see you, every time. I just wanted you to know, in case you already didn't, that I love you."

Ìní's response was to place both her hands over her eyes, she was too overwrought to speak. Faison stood there holding her by her folded arms. Afterwards, when she moved her hands away, her eyes were streaming with tears.

He walked her home in silence. He didn't question her quiet mood, he was in a reflective one of his own.

Chapter 15

2015

I hate this corner of East London, Ìní thought, as she skipped over yet another puddle filled with cigarettes and eyed the youths across the road. They were gathered over what she assumed was weed, otherwise she couldn't really fathom what the huddle was about. They were all dressed in black with lace-up shoes and skinny jeans, the current uniform of creatives.

Sometimes she wondered if her lack of means in getting "the uniform" had held her back in artistic or literary circles. She almost wished her purse strings would stretch far enough to allow her to dress more freely.

She walked past the building and didn't realise.

When the road ended and she came to a crossroads with a bottle-green warehouse across from her, she knew she had gone too far. There were no more house numbers. She furrowed her eyebrows, grabbed the front of her afro hair nervously and started to walk back.

Her phone rang.

It was Faison.

She debated whether to pick it up. It would either give her nervous energy or bulk her up for the meeting. She decided on the latter.

"Hello?"

"Are you there yet?" Faison asked.

"Ìní? Ninology...? I can hear you breathing, is that you?" he questioned repeatedly.

"Yes, yes I'm here. I'm ok. I walked past the place. I'm nervous, ok? Call me after."

"Ok, good luck. Be yourself. You'll be great."

"Thanks." She hung up.

Ìní looked to her right and found that she'd arrived at the door. It was marked 'DHF agency' but there was no number.

She looked down at her shoes, breathed in deeply, then glanced at her watch. She was still fifteen minutes early. She rang the bell corresponding to DHF agency to the left. A robotic voice said, 'Come in' then buzzed her in.

She briefly wondered how trusting they must be in this building to buzz her in blindly, then remembered there was a reflective black circle above all the signs. That must've been the camera.

She briefly wondered if she looked ok, then decided it was too late anyway.

She walked in to reception, greeted the young guy there, and took a seat where he pointed.

After about twenty minutes, Shirley herself came out to get her and introduced herself warmly. She was clearly busy, she walked very fast and talked even faster.

Ìní got the sense Shirley was very intelligent and missed out words because her brain moved faster than her mouth. An incongruent quality for a book editor if she ever saw one.

As she followed Shirley down the narrow halls, she took in the bright offices and marvelled at the messy yet manicured stacks on all the desks. *Shirley must run a tight ship*, Ìní thought.

"Ìní...!"

"Er, huh! I'm sorry. Yes," she spluttered.

"I said how long have you been writing?"

"All my life really. As long as I can remember."

They walked towards an office at the end of the corridor. There was a sign on the door saying Shirley-Ann Cottage Birder Flouser. It was even brighter in the office. Ìní liked it immediately. She sat down after Shirley had taken her seat.

Ìní looked up, ready for an interrogation.

"So, you met Josh at one of our trade shows?"

"Yes."

"Look, I'll be honest with you. I like your book and we want to publish it but you have to go through a few rewrites. There's a few – it's just easier if I show you my notes."

Shirley swivelled left on her chair, then stretched about three-quarters of the way towards the papers piled on her left and pulled out Ìní's draft.

On the front page, was a list in red pen. Ìní assumed that was the 'what's-wrong' list. Shirley ran through the list, they agreed on a deadline and Ìní, unable to hide her joy, agreed to go and rework the draft.

After the meeting, on her way out, she waved to Josh the assistant and made her way out the building.

By the time she got out, her toes were sweating and she had to sit down as they were slipping out onto the street in her summer sandals.

She sat in a nearby doorway and fanned herself with the manuscript. She contemplated what to do or whom to call first. She decided to celebrate privately and focus on how much work she had to do first.

She called the cafe and asked if she could take the rest of the week off. Her boss, Norma, disagreed and told her to find someone to cover her shifts instead. She thought about Blessed and her numerous cousins, and how many favours Blessed owed her from taking time off to go to all their weddings. She immediately called Blessed.

Blessed picked up but she was in the middle of a sewing session, it seemed this one would last all night, there was another wedding. She agreed to take four out of the five of Ìní's shifts for the rest of the week so Ìní could work on her draft. Ìní thanked Blessed and hung up.

Ìní skipped all the way to the tube, head buried in the draft, mentally ticking off lists of requests by Shirley. Some of the notes were questions from Josh to Shirley – illegible and eye-strain inducing, but Ìní was grateful for the attention they paid to her writing.

———

"Daddy, how is it living back in Nigeria?"

"It's ok. I miss your mother."

"Then why are you living there? Just come back. She's pretty unhappy too," said Ìní.

"I am unhappy when I'm over there," said Ernest.

"What about your contracts? Mum says you moved back because of your NYSC contracts."

"That did not materialise. Simon…uh, look, Simon lied. By the way, congratulations on finding a publisher.

I'm so sorry I tried to force you into something else. I was worried all our efforts and sacrifice would be in vain if you didn't do something that was a sure thing."

"It's ok and I got there in the end. They're a small publisher." Ìní paused slightly and waited for the interference on the phone line to be over before she continued, "You know, I also realise the pursuit of passions is a luxury. If I had stayed in Nigeria, this wouldn't even be an option for people like us." After a small pause, during which Ernest said nothing. He could always tell when his quiet daughter was going to say more. "Thank you for everything you did for us, for giving up your dream so we could have one," she finally added.

"There is that saying..."

"What saying, Dad?"

"There are two greatest days in a human's life, the day they're born and the day they find out why. My happiest times was when I was running my bookshop and when I was supplying books to the NYSC. Like you, I loved books and even when I was doing something adjacent, I was happy. I'm glad that you have that now."

"So, the problem isn't Mummy but that life wasn't flowing through you," said Ìní.

There was a long silence on the line and the crackling on the end of Ernest's line was the only thing heard above their breathing. "Exactly," Ernest said, ending the silence.

———

Ernest had taken to calling Grace on Sundays, ostensibly to get an update on his children, but really it was to hear her voice.

She didn't know that, so she always made sure she had something to tell him so he wouldn't think she was not interested in the daily lives of her children.

One evening, they ended up talking for an hour and she found herself looking forward to his calls more and more.

Another evening, he didn't call so she got out all his letters that she had saved and read them. She noticed he signed off most of them with 'Still in love with you'. At the time, she had taken them for granted, but now she relished those words and read them again and again, wondering if he still felt that way. From what she could tell, he spent most of his time at the house and wasn't dating anyone. His stories revolved around going out to buy food or petrol, and spending time with his sister, who had some domestic problems with her husband.

Chapter 16

2010, Surrey, UK

Ìkẹmi had luminous brown skin that reflected light perfectly. While others struggled with teenage acne, her rich brown skin was perfectly poreless. She carried it off with a certain lightness, because she was mostly unaware of her beauty, and on the days she felt she looked good, she didn't pay it much attention beyond the morning glance in the mirror. Her glowing chocolate-coloured eyes made it seem like she could draw you into their whirlpool warmth.

The first boy to be mesmerised by Ìkẹmi was Luke Traynor in middle school. Luke was short with light brown hair that fell over his forehead, highlighting his gentle hazel eyes. He had a certain confidence from his loving, effusive hippie parents. He had a sister who was two years older, who told him secrets behind the behaviour of girls, plus he played netball on the girls' team because after years of watching his sister play, he had cajoled the gym teacher into letting him play too.

Luke and Ìkẹmi's friendship started when he started asking about her life back in Nigeria. Feeling confused about his questions on what the roads, houses and other mundane stuff were like, Ìkẹmi furnished him with great tall tales of impossible things. His suburban Surrey life paling in comparison, he followed her around, mesmerised by her voice and quick Lagos accent. Before long, they were inseparable and Ìkẹ́mi spent Friday nights with Luke's family, having dinner with them and listening to the Traynors' evening ritual. His parents, James and Gardenia, played games after dinner, then argued about politics of years gone by, which was in stark contrast to her parents who had not been in the same country for years. His older sister, Muffie, would be locked in her room with her girlfriends after dinner, discussing which stickers of boyband members they would like to collect from the magazines the following week.

Over the course of her first school year in England, Ìkẹ́mi started to love the way Luke adored her, and shortly after she developed a crush on him too. She loved the way his bowl haircut fell into his eyes. She also loved his hazel eyes when he was being gullible and lapping up her elaborate stories.

At the end of middle school, he wrote in her notebook. His square handwriting leaving imprints on the subsequent blank sheets in her notebook.

Ikemi, I loved you from Day one in school. Thanks for sharing your stories and teaching me Yoruba. I hope we stay in touch in secondary school. Mum says you are always welcome for Friday night dinners.

Love u,

Luke

Their friendship had ended abruptly one Monday afternoon, when meeting after secondary school, she had found out his full name was Larkspur after she had revealed her full name as Ìkẹ́misọla. Not familiar with non-tropical plant names outside of hibiscus and roses, she had laughed and wounded Luke's pride.

But the puppy love he had for her had cemented the way she would like to be loved – completely adored and worshipped. Thus, she first dated Ládoyè, not because of his family, his money or his good looks but because she liked the way he loved her.

Thus, it was always a surprise to Ìní how Ìkẹ́mi was the only one always visiting Ládoyè in Abuja. She saved up all her holidays for August and would go visit him. She had done that for years throughout their university days.

Still, Ìkẹ́mi was Ìní's biggest supporter so she always tried to support her in turn.

———

"What was it our parents' generation used to say? Something about a lizard...?" she clicked her fingers trying to snap it back into remembrance. "You can't clothe a lizard," Ìkẹ́mi finally said, eyes bright with the epiphany.

"They don't say that! I think you mean, 'you can't polish a turd' and there is no such saying in Yorùbá," Ìní said laughing and wiping tears on her sleeve.

"O ò lè fáláàngbá láṣọ. I'm sure my mum used to say it, and it's true too. You can't put clothes on a lizard, they have no shoulders."

They were on their way to a party in Windsor, one of Ìní's old friends had invited them. Having blitzed their way through a bottle of wine with a small dinner, they were now on the train with Ìkẹ́mi trying not to slur her words and making Ìní laugh with her usual words of wisdom.

"Let's play, what-if-he-was-bald," Ìkẹ́mi said.

They played their old university game where they picked out handsome men and imagined if they would still be dateable if bald. They played until the train reached its destination.

Ìní tried not to talk about Faison too much except to complain once, "He lives in East London, deep east. I feel like I'm dating long distance. I'm going to dump him."

"If you want," Ìkẹ́mi said, not unkindly, but also not taking the bait.

After the train pulled into Windsor and Eton station, Ìkẹ́mi stopped to look at her reflection on an empty billboard. A couple walked past them with the guy carrying several bags of shopping while the woman carried nothing. Observing them, Ìkẹ́mi said, "You know how well you treat them is how good they'll keep looking," Ìkẹ́mi said, adjusting her skirt to face backwards.

"What do you mean?" Ìní said, looking down at her own skirt and making adjustments. *Should I be wearing this backwards too?* She thought.

"If you want to know an unhappy marriage, look at the woman. A bad marriage shows on the woman more not the man, my mum looked terrible for years until she finally left Dad and moved to England. Technically, they're still married. I call it the modern divorce, move to another country." Ìkẹ́mi laughed but not altogether happily. She applied another coat of lipstick and started walking ahead.

Ìní switched her skirt back quickly. With the shirt tail still hanging out, she ran after Ìkẹ́mi to keep up.

———

At the party, a guy was leaning heavily towards Ìkẹ́mi and hitting on her but she kept moving away and wouldn't engage him. He was a peripheral friend from university whom they hadn't seen in the intervening years.

"Why didn't you want to talk to Matthew tonight?" Ìní asked Ìkẹ́mi later on the way home.

"Because I think he was hitting on me. Besides, that other girl who was asking about your hair liked him, I think."

"People have a lot of opinions about black women's hair. If you straighten it, if you have it natural, if you braid it or if you have extensions, someone has an opinion."

"Yeah, and let's face it, she's no chicken."

"I think the saying is 'she's no spring chicken'," Ìní said laughing.

"Whatever," Ìkẹ́mi waved her hands dismissively. "Who is she to say your hairstyle is old fashioned? I don't think she was very nice."

"Why didn't you give Matthew a chance?" Ìní said.

"Because of Ládoyè."

"What about Ládoyè? He never calls you back. He doesn't answer your texts."

"I told you he hates text messaging. He's not good on his phone."

"Didn't you say he works in tech?"

"I said his dad owns a tech company."

"So, he's not good with texting or calling. Don't you find that a little bit weird?"

"Like your relationship is perfect!" Ìkẹ́mi yelled.

"I'm not saying my relationship is perfect. But at least I know where I stand with Faison even if I don't always understand his odd French ways."

The train had now pulled up to the platform at the station. Ìkẹ́mi started walking ahead rapidly to sit in the furthest carriage, Ìní followed unsure whether her friend wanted to sit alone on the way home. Ìní caught up with her and they ended up sitting opposite each other in a four-seater alcove.

Ìní leaned forward and said gently, "I'm just saying if a friend did any of those things that Ládoyè does, you would not consider that person a friend. If you called me and I never answered and you texted me and I never answered. But occasionally, when I felt like it, I would text you and tell you how much I love you and what you mean to me, completely expecting you to forget my behaviour, we would not be friends. So why would you accept that behaviour from a boyfriend if you wouldn't accept it from me? Think about it."

"You would never guess who I ran into?" Ìní said.

"Who?" Démì said.

"Your ex-girlfriend, Mia. She's Faison's friend from when he lived in Amsterdam."

"What?"

"Did you know she wrote a book about her father after he passed away?"

"I knew her father passed away but I didn't know she wrote a book."

"Yeah, she did. Her father was an illegal immigrant in the Netherlands and when he died, she went there to retrace his steps and wrote about it."

"Oh my God. How did I not know that?"

"Because you're too busy pontificating about your ideals," Ìní said.

After a short pause, Démì said, "Did she ask about me?"

"We didn't talk about you much actually. She did ask if you were living with Dad in Nigeria, which I took to mean, were you living with a woman?"

"You think?" Démì said, he sat up in bed hopefully.

"Well, I would say it's a safe bet she still cares about you. I mean you guys were together for what, a year?"

"Yeah, just under a year but I miss her every day. I've been meaning to write to her. Do you think I should?"

"All I can say is, if you're going to, you'd better have something to say."

———

Ernest hadn't left the house all day. The carpenter came and then the electrician and each one was more incompetent than the last. He missed how things worked in England and wished he could just pay and have something work.

He had wanted to install solar panels but the two charlatans he spoke to had convinced him perhaps this was a tall order for now.

His life revolved around chores around the house and his weekly conversations with Grace. It reminded him of their years of separation when she had first started working in England and he was taking care of the kids in Nigeria. *Who knew that would now be the good old days*? Still, he wondered how she felt about their separation, she was hard to read in person and even more so on the phone.

And then in the midst of all his heartbreak and crisis with Grace, Yẹyè died.

———

"Helloooo? Grace! Can you hear me?"

"Ernest, yes I can hear you."

"My younger sister Yẹyè has died o!"

"Ehn, Auntie Yẹyè. Say it isn't so. Ọkọ mi ooooo." Grace cried. This was followed by a long silence on Ernest's side. He was briefly taken aback by Grace's use of his old nickname. They were not officially divorced but she had stopped calling him that months before he moved back to Àkúrẹ́ and it was jarring for him to hear the nickname again – *my husband* – he mulled over the literal meaning in his mind. So simple, yet it always touched his heart. She had first started calling him that after he proposed and hearing it always melted his heart, especially when that idiot Doctor was still hanging around her family back in the village, hoping to make Grace his second wife.

Eventually, he recovered from his long gaze into the past, to tell Grace about the funeral details. *Was she coming?*

No, she responded sadly, she couldn't get the time off work and the flights would be too expensive so close to the funeral.

The funeral was a sombre affair. Ìní had sent a poem about a eucalyptus tree that reminded her of Yẹyè. Ernest wasn't certain what it all meant except that Yẹyè's skin reminded Ìní of weeping eucalyptus trees, amber liquid oozing from her pores like her skin was full and it needed to let go of some liquid to breathe again. Ernest thought, but wasn't sure, that Ìní's elegy was in reference to all the times Yẹyè showed up at the house with congealed blood on her face, having been beaten by her husband again. He was afraid to ask Ìní because to do so was to make it true.

Ernest's own memories of his sister was her winning hospitality. His children had found her bullish but it was because with so little control over her own life, she had tried to control them and fill Grace's shoes at the same time, but the bullish and forced maternal behaviour was altogether unpalatable to them.

At a loss what to say for the eulogy, he spoke of the time they had gone to her house and with what little she had, she had tried to make them comfortable.

"She'd offered you a drink before you sat down. She knew which of the mismatched seats in her house would fit your personality. The straight-backed wooden seat for my son, Démì, the sunken blue sofa for my daughter, Ìní, and the rough yellow love seat at the end of the room for me. She would sit on the bed and watch us all enjoy the afternoon as it passed into evening. She had no electricity in her place. No bulbs. But in the long face-me-I-face-you hallway, some of the lights from the other bedsits lining the hallway, would filter through and light the small room. She'd leave the door open knowing it meant we couldn't stay for much longer because of the mosquitoes. She would leave the door open so Ìní could still read her big-lettered children's books. I couldn't save her from her husband but I did everything I could. I'm sorry."

Chapter 17

"I should be feeling accomplished and sensified now that I've broken up with Ládoyè," Ìkẹ́mi said.

"Er, you mean sensible? Ìní said. They were at their favourite Korean fried chicken place.

"No, I mean sensified, full of sense. Not uncertain and filled with terror, like I'm feeling now."

"Thank you so much for reading my poem, by the way."

"You're welcome," Ìkẹ́mi said. "It is hard when someone who bullied you dies."

"Apart from that, she was also very kind and I finally realised the reason she was so bullish. Of course, it took me years to understand that the stuff on her face, when she would show up at our house, was in fact congealed blood. I put it together one evening watching one of those American cop shows. The latent picture in my memory all just precipitated in that moment that, I've seen this before," Ìní said.

"Yeah, it also made me realise what I was going through with Ládoyè. That raw bleeding wound that was my heart each time he hurt me. Even though it's my heart and not my body involved. It's still abuse and it hurts. In many ways, I realise the heart takes longer to heal," said Ìkẹ́mi.

"Yeah, if you don't die first like my aunt Yẹyè," Ìní said reaching for some kimchi.

———

Démì had to go to Bariga for a client meeting. He was reticent about the long journey across town so he went out to tell his driver to get the car ready. They would leave just before sunrise.

He looked up, looks like it would rain today, so traffic may be bad.

Getting back into the house to put his socks on, along with the rest of his outfit, he tried to hurry so he could beat the traffic especially on the third mainland bridge.

As he walked into the office later, Tósìn, his assistant greeted him warmly. He smiled to himself, it seemed her sunny side was up today. The surly assistant was a good indication of how the day would go.

"Help me call Mr Adéníyan," he said to her, then walked into his office to take off his jacket. His back was already covered in sweat. He became aware of a presence behind him, Mr Ajax had followed him in and was standing by the door with his hands in his pockets waiting for Démì to turn around.

"Is this the only plant you have here?" Mr Ajax asked.

"Good afternoon, sir," Démì replied. "No, well we had to take one of them out, it was attracting flies."

"Ok, well... em what are you doing for lunch?" Mr Ajax asked after what seemed like an age, the silence stretching between them into an awkward stand-off.

Démì had learned to get comfortable with the long silences his boss created, figuring he always said what he came for eventually. He never used phones, instead preferring to walk down all twenty-two floors to Démì's office.

"I have no lunch meetings today so I'm free," Démì said.

"Let's get ready, we have a new client. He's from Peckham."

Démì found it absurd when they wheeled him out every time they had a new client claiming to be from London.

He nodded. After another long pause, Mr Ajax turned and walked away. His pointy-toed shoes echoing down the tiled hallway.

For lunch, they went to an Italian restaurant, it was close to the office so they walked down Ìlárá road.

Outside the joint, drivers were lounging in cars with their seats reclined waiting for their bosses to finish returning from the popular lunch spot.

He spotted a familiar face. It was the taxi driver from his first night in Lagos who had stolen his stuff, he thought briefly about going to confront him but then he'd have to explain to Mr Ajax. He didn't want to risk another silent stand-off while explaining so instead he followed his boss into the restaurant to meet their new client.

After the meeting, it turned out the client only wanted to talk about how much money he had made in London and how to invest it in Nigeria.

When he found out Démì used to live in Finchley, he went quiet on his bragging and focused intently on his catfish.

Advising the client that wasn't their forte, they left the restaurant shortly after. On their walk back to the office, he asked Mr Ajax if he could have time off, he wanted to go to London for his little sister's wedding.

"Oh, you have a sister?" Mr Ajax said turning to face him and beaming. Sweat running down his wide forehead and dripping between his enormous glasses.

"Yes, sir. I do," Démì said.

"Your parents must be very proud of you. Your sister is getting married and now you a lawyer. That's a good family."

"I have a daughter myself, you know," he continued after they had silently crossed two streets and were now in foyer of their cool offices.

"How's your brother?" Ìkẹ́mi said.

"Don't think Démì is having much luck dating in Lagos. I think the culture shock is getting to him and there is a significant cultural difference, which is weird because he thinks he hasn't changed."

"Maybe, he's looking for a bimbo. Women are much more complicated than men think they are, and men are much less complicated than we think they are," Ìkẹ́mi said, chewing on a piece of gum.

"I don't know what he's looking for. Anyway, he's coming for my wedding."

"That's great. You know, I saw him in Lagos?" Ìkẹ́mi said.

"Oh really? He mentioned you two might catch up."

"He was really boring. He kept asking me about Mia and I got the impression he didn't like Ládoyè. I was still with Ládoyè then and for once, he came down from Abuja and we all went out to dinner, they didn't get on at all. So uncomfortable. Maybe that should've been a clue. Ládoyè sees all men as competition."

Chapter 18

Dear Mia,

I suppose I have no right to contact you like this. How are you?

I'm doing well. I've been living in Lagos and working for a law firm here. It is fun, if not a total culture shock.

I realised I was unfair to you in my demands regarding our cultural differences. Being an ethnic minority is hard enough without the complicated additional layers of the expectations we put on each other and for that, I am sorry.

I'll be coming to London town in August for Ìní's wedding. Would you care to go for some coffee and cake? You can have coffee while I have the cake, just like we used to.

ps. I miss you. Please give me another chance.

Love,

Démì

Mia had been ruminating on Démì's words since he left London. After meeting Ìní and being inspired by the way she lived her truth fully. It reminded her of when she first met Faison in Amsterdam. Even then, as a young guy, it had struck her how he unabashedly embraced all parts of himself – his Congolese dialect sneaking out when teasing his friends, and when he got mad, swearing without reserve in Parisian vernacular. She decided to go back to being called by her first name, Efua, and with it went her email and her name at work – the HR lady had been most confused and had grilled her as to why she was changing her name, was she getting married?

Despite all the questions, HR had changed it to Mia Efua Kwateng, instead of just plain Efua Kwateng, which had prompted Mia to go back again to have it changed properly. In the interim, she'd missed a few emails and it had caused quite the commotion at work.

Now after a few weeks, she was feeling more at peace with her new name. Mia was her middle name and apart from her father, no one else called her that back home and it should remain that way. It was time to live in her full truth. Her father would have wanted it that way.

"Wow, what a day! You are getting married, and to a non-Naija. I still don't know how you swung that one with the parents." Démì adjusted his tie in the mirror. He didn't feel better. He was still overheating.

"I know! He's a great guy. He's easy to like," Ìní said.

"I remember when you said he first met Mum, and he ate ẹ̀bà with a fork," Démì laughed.

"The way she looked at me! Like who have you brought home to me?" Ìní said. But when we went to meet Dad in Àkúrẹ́. Dad, sweet as can be, saw his goodness. It was game over."

Switching tack Démì said, "And I see your arrogant friend is here. I saw her outside, she didn't even greet me. Pah!!!!"

"Ìkẹ́mi is not arrogant, she's just rich."

"Yeah, rich in rudeness. I know her family, they lack manners."

"Says the one who lives in Ikoyi. You are also rolling with rich people so you're not one to judge."

"True. I got into it with the guy at the airport who was hostile because I was leaving the country with a British passport."

"Why, did he want a bribe?"

"Not when I asked him. Apparently, he thought it was people like me who are stealing from the country because we are apparently rich. I wanted to give him a lecture about who is really stealing from him. Instead, I just told him, my parents just found a way to leave when things got really tough. Dad worked as a cleaner for years."

"Yeah, can you believe how far we've come?" said Ìní.

"Yeah, not at all actually. How's jittery Joe?"

"Don't call him that. He's just a nervous person. Actually, go and check on him, please. He'll be expecting you."

"Ok, where are you two going for your honeymoon?"

"We're going to visit famous libraries in Europe."

"Of course, you are," Démì said sarcastically.

"Please go and find Faison and try to calm him down, pleeeeease?"

"Ok, ok," raising both hands and smiling, Démì backed away and turned to leave the room.

Démì sat down in front. Someone nudged him to his left, then he realised he was sitting next to Faison's mother. *Oh, he was in the wrong seat.*

He got up.

He sat down again.

This time in the right place.

It was hard to breathe.

One…

Two...

Three…

Why was she here? How did she get an invite? Did she know he was coming? She looked beautiful. He had to find Ìní. True to form, she would be the last to arrive. As the bride should. He wanted to look back but he couldn't.

The organist had started playing. It was time for duties. He got up to stand next to Xavier, Faison's brother. He took a chance and looked back, maybe it wasn't her after all.

No, it definitely was, and she was wearing the wedding theme colours.

Xavier was now whispering something to him. He must've said it a few times and been ignored by Démì's internal turmoil because now he was looking annoyed and gesturing wildly with his left hand.

Oh, here comes the bride.

Breathe.

"Thank you all for coming," Ernest began his speech. "We are very proud of our daughter Ìníọláolúwa," Grace jabbed him in the leg. He was always forgetting and adding the extra suffix 'Olúwa' to Ìní's name, forgetting they had agreed to name her the far simpler Ìníọlá.

"Ahem, Ìníọlá," Ernest corrected himself. "Ìníọlá is what we named her. As some of you who are Yorùbá here know, we like to add God in some way to our children's names," Ernest chuckled. "We thank God today for the union of Fezohn and Ìní." Ernest in his tonal Yorùbá accent still could not manage to pronounce his new son-in-law's name. "Grace and myself have been married for almost 40 years so it is our pleasure to see our darling daughter here today getting married hoping she too will enjoy a long matrimony as her mother and I have done. We came to this country many years ago with nothing to our name. We took a gamble because we wanted a better life for our children and today I am very happy to say, one of them is a lawyer after moving back to Lagos and the other, the bride today is a writer with her first book of poems coming out next month." The wedding guests erupted with applause.

"What am I saying?" Ernest continued. "Without us coming here, Ìní and Faison would never have met and with our circumstances back home before we left, we would not be where we are today so glory to God. So, raise your glasses with me for a toast to Fezohn and Ìní."

"To Faison and Ìní," the guests said in unison.

Epilogue

At the book launch, Faison stood at the back of the room and watched her read. It was the one about how they met.

He was late so he didn't get a seat.

He stood wedged between two other guys that had cycled in, so they were sweating too.

As the sweat on his brow dried, he smiled as he listened to her familiar voice read.

"Your love wraps me up,

Like sitting in a tree,

When the tracks are down and deep within me..."

Line by line, with the graceful cadence that had always drawn him in when she spoke.

Something about it always calmed him.

It was like it matched the beat of his heart.

His ubiquitous nervousness, which was only still when he was alone, was gone. His jittery right knee settled down into its socket.

He listened with his whole body, he listened like she spoke only to him.

Acknowledgements

Dedicated to the memory of CK, who personified grace under fire.

Dedicated to superman, for always believing in us, for never giving up on us. To borrow Base's words 'You will never find the bottom of our love for you'.

And to the ever effervescent Felup, I am without enough words, but for now I hope 'thank you' will do.

More books by Lola R. Opeyemi

Look out for these titles from the same author.

The Secrets in the Walls – coming in 2022

Manoah was one of the lost children of the foster care "farming" generation of the 1960s, given away by his Nigerian parents so they could pursue their dreams of a career in London.

But what happens when his foster mother, Mercedes, tries to keep him for good? And what about Ophelia Mayberry, the girl next door whom he falls for while he's living with Mercedes?

When a secret threatens to destroy the foster home and its residents, Manoah is forced to leave. But what happens to the love of his life, Ophelia, and the other children?

The Secrets in the Walls is a story of courage and what it means to love with your whole heart.

Printed in Great Britain
by Amazon

81411308R00140